A RUNNING JUMP

Recent Titles by Gerald Hammond

FINE TUNE *
FOLLOW THAT GUN
MAD DOGS AND SCOTSMEN
PARADE'S END
SINK OR SWIM
STING IN THE TAIL

* *available from Severn House*

A RUNNING JUMP

Gerald Hammond

This first world edition published in Great Britain 1998 by
SEVERN HOUSE PUBLISHERS LTD of
9–15 High Street, Sutton, Surrey SM1 1DF.
This first world edition published in the U.S.A. 1999 by
SEVERN HOUSE PUBLISHERS INC of
595 Madison Avenue, New York, N.Y. 10022.

British Library Cataloguing in Publication Data

Hammond, Gerald, 1926-
    A running jump
    1. Detective and mystery stories
    I. Title
    823.9'14 [F]   MYS

    ISBN 0-7278-2233-0   1069587

Typeset by Hewer Text Ltd,
Edinburgh, Scotland.
Printed and bound in Great Britain by
MPG Books Ltd, Bodmin, Cornwall.

One

Ever afterwards, Polly James knew that that was the moment from which the rest of her life would date.

"No, no, no," her mother said, too loudly. "I just don't believe you."

"Don't then," Polly retorted, tight-lipped. "It's true all the same. I'm going. He told me to take a running jump and that's what I'm going to do. Until I get out of here, just keep him away from me."

She climbed the stairs to the bright bedroom which suddenly looked unfamiliar. She had a haversack left from a camping holiday a year earlier and into it she crammed her few spare clothes. Almost as an afterthought she found room for a stuffed animal of uncertain breed, her night-time comfort over the years.

Descending again, very quietly, she heard voices from the equally small sitting room, her mother's gentle voice – too 'posh', she thought again, for this rural neighbourhood – and a man's voice raised defensively, the latest in a long line of 'uncles'. She had time for a quick visit to the kitchen.

At the click of the front door latch her mother came out. They faced each other on the path of crazy paving where weeds and rock plants pushed through. "You'd

Gerald Hammond

better go to your aunt Maud," her mother said, still loudly.

"I suppose so," Polly said. *Like hell!* she added silently. Her aunt, a patrician lady with an affectionate but authoritarian manner, lived in a stuffy house in a stuffy street and Polly hated her. She had been sent to stay with her aunt when her father died suddenly of an unsuspected heart condition, and she had felt as if she was being suffocated in eiderdowns.

Her mother lowered her voice. "Next time a man makes a pass at you, take it as a compliment. Don't grab for the bread knife."

"It was a steak knife I meant to get hold of."

"Much more suitable but likely to land you in trouble. Try throwing the crockery. It's noisy and expensive and the law looks on crockery-throwing as a female privilege. Well, I'll see you when I see you."

As she pulled the gate to behind her and set off between the trees, Polly thought that she never knew whether her mother meant the things she said. On the whole, she probably did, but along with a host of corollaries which she felt went without saying.

Back in the house, the man was saying, "She's really gone this time?" He was plump and silver-haired and he had a moustache which Polly had always felt sure must be actionable at law.

"It would seem so, thanks to you." Polly's mother – she remained officially Mrs Turnbull – lit a cigarette and blew smoke at the ceiling. "Can't you keep your hands to yourself for one minute? She's only seventeen, for God's sake!"

"That's right. She's just a child. I was only going to let her sit on my knee for a moment."

2

"Don't whine, especially while you're lying. She'll be eighteen in a few days. Half her contemporaries have babies by now, but that's not what I want for her. I may not be all that I should be, but I'm certainly not having her turned into my clone. God, does she have any money, to get to her aunt's? I forgot to ask." She hurried through into the kitchen, a larger room than the sitting room and surprisingly up to date. She found her handbag but the purse had disappeared. Stretching, she reached down the Wedgwood teapot from the top shelf. That too was empty.

"The little cow," she called to the man. "She's cleaned me out. Rent money, telephone money, the lot." She darted outside but there was no sign of her daughter.

Polly glanced back once at the creeper-clad former farmhouse and then set off in her loose-limbed stride. She paused and waited in the security of a tumble-down shed for a few minutes The autumn afternoon was warm and that place had been her favourite refuge from all the complications of teenage life, so she was not uncomfortable. When she could be sure that there was to be no pursuit she resumed her walking.

She wondered as she walked what the future might bring. She was prepared to face it without trepidation. She was giving up a promised place at university, but what else? The uncertain security of life with a mother who, since the death of Polly's father when she was only entering her teens, had sought the protection of any man prepared to keep herself and her daughter in a certain style. She had even married one of them, a Henry Turnbull, but it hadn't lasted. (When that relationship had been on its last legs, Polly recalled her mother telling

3

the world that the name had originally been Trumble, a short form of Gutrumble.) Polly did not blame her mother for her adopted lifestyle. A combination of unlucky breaks and bad judgements had left them penniless when her father died and her mother had no other talent to exploit. But she herself had no inclination for the life of the odalisque. She had no experience of sex beyond the occasional fumbled petting with a classmate, but had a feeling that performing the act, as she imagined it, without love would be repellent. With Polly off her hands, perhaps her mother might become more like other mothers. Not absolutely like them, Polly thought, because other mothers were dull and boring and as repressive as her aunt, but she might incline a little bit in that direction.

For the rest, Polly thought, she could at last give up those damned dance lessons. She had absolute confidence in her own ability to think her way through any problems that might arise.

Ten minutes brought her to the main road. Her newly matured body, she knew, was not unattractive to men. She had a good figure and was determined to take care of it. But her school clothes must have been a deterrent. Car after car hesitated and then swept past. In her blazer pocket she felt her mother's small vegetable knife and checked again that the sharp point was still embedded in the old champagne cork. Any driver trying it on would have a shock coming.

The first vehicle to pull up was a large van carrying vegetables for the early-morning market in the city. Polly climbed aboard.

"Where do you want to go?" the driver asked.

"Into the city. Can you drop me at the station?" she asked. "I'm heading for London."

The driver was drooping man nearing pensionable age and no threat to a young girl. He had another silver moustache, but somehow this one was quite forgivable. "You don't want to go to London," he said. "London's no place for the likes of you."

"I'm going to stay with my aunt," she said. It was almost true. It was where her mother wanted her to go.

"Oh." For a moment, the driver was disarmed. Then he brightened up. He was never so happy as when he was prophesying doom. "You shouldn't be running around alone at this time of day, a young girl like you. And the last train will've gone."

That seemed unlikely. "I'm being met," Polly said.

"I hope so. But they'll have a long wait. I've more collections to do along the way. And I don't go near the station."

"Drop me wherever's nearest."

As they rumbled through the harvest-filled country-side, Polly listened with half an ear to an endless lecture about the dangers to be faced by a young girl. He sounded so indignant that Polly began to wonder if he regretted not being one of them. Polly, who had a lively sense of humour, saw him as a challenge and set out to make him laugh.

It was soon clear that his prediction had been sound. They made several calls at market gardens. Polly would have got out and looked for a swifter lift except that they had left the main roads for the rural B-roads. They ran between tall hedges and through tunnels formed by ancient trees. The daylight slipped away but

5

she held herself in patience. She had no appointments until eternity. One hour was as good as another.

There would be no point, the driver explained at length, in arriving at the market before it opened in the early hours. They stopped at a small café where he seemed to be well known and they drank tea and ate bacon sandwiches for which Polly, as recipient of the favour, found that she was expected to pay.

Her customary bedtime was imminent. Polly had passed some hours surfing on the excitement of her sudden rebellion. But such moods can never be maintained indefinitely. Now she was content to drift along with events. When they took to the road again she dozed in the uncomfortable bucket seat. The sound of the engine became remote. The rocking of their stately progress through the darkness became the motion of the boat on the river, two or three uncles ago. Soon she was sound asleep.

When she awoke, they were in city streets and the van had come to a halt. "Here you are," he said. "This is as near the station as I go. It's somewhere down there, I think," he added, pointing. "But the last train's gone. I *told* you it would."

"That's quite all right," she said politely. "And thank you very much." She still had not made him laugh. Perhaps nobody ever would.

She grabbed her haversack and climbed out. The van drove off. Polly, gradually wakening, looked around her. She was standing on a corner where an intersection of five streets created a small square or plaza having, at its centre, a paved area with a statue of some dignitary who, Polly thought, to judge from his clothes, was probably long dead and from his expression, just as well. The square was adequately lit, although by lamps which tinted living flesh with the colour of death, but the street which the van driver had indicated was narrow, gloomy and somehow menacing.

Not far away, a building was showing an illuminated entrance. Polly headed in that direction. The building turned out to be a hotel. Polly approached the door. The hotel did not seem to be pretentious, but the prices of rooms were quoted on a small notice beside the doorway and they stopped Polly in her tracks. One night at that price and her small, ill-gotten hoard would be almost gone. Did people really pay such prices? She had only a vague idea what the train fare to London might be, but she doubted very much that it would still be within her remaining means.

The only other building spilling light turned out to be a small café, even smaller than the one that they had visited at the roadside. With the appetite of youth, Polly's stomach had already forgotten about one small round of bacon sandwiches several hours earlier.

In the café, several youths were snickering around a corner table while a man yawned behind a counter which looked reasonably clean. Polly was usually fastidious about healthy eating but for once she might allow herself a second bout of junk food. She paid for a large mug of tea, a hot dog and a meat pie and sat down to review her situation. At first, this did not seem to give many grounds for optimism and she was in half a mind to phone her mother or even her aunt for help. But by the time the tea, the pie and the hot dog had warmed and comforted her, she was more inclined to look on the brighter side. One was not allowed to starve in Britain today. There was probably a law about it, or if not, then something would turn up. With this Micawberish thought came another. Surely the coaches ran through the night? And they would be cheaper than the trains, she was almost sure. What was more, if she had missed the last one there would surely be somewhere warm and sheltered where she could wait out the night.

The youths had gone, only the man was left and he was tidying up. He gave her directions to the bus depot, which turned out to be next to the railway station and to be approached along the unattractive street pointed out by the van driver.

The night, when she went out into it, was colder. Several cars went by as she left the café and then all was quiet. Spookily quiet, she thought, as if everyone were deliberately looking the other way. Her footsteps, usually inaudible, echoed around the empty space as she walked towards the corner. The street leading towards the station seemed more menacing than ever. She paused under the last street lamp, hesitating before the darkness. It was a relief when she heard other footsteps. She looked round. The four youths were approaching.

Her first thought was that they might escort her to the bus station. Her second was that she might have been safer alone. They were a rough looking group, the roughness not the result of hard work or poor education but carefully cultivated. Their hair was universally cropped and greasy, partly covered by baseball caps worn back to front. Tattered jeans and matching denim jackets painted with alarming crests and slogans were worn with heavy boots to complete the ensemble. She thought it was probably a sort of uniform, as members of the great underclass of those who had opted out.

The four formed a barrier round her, isolating her against the window of an estate agent. She could smell sweat and several variants of male aftershave and deodorant but there was something else which instinct recognised as the excitement of the hunter approaching prey.

"Hullo, darling," said the leader.

Polly kept her head. She decided that an appeal to their better natures would cost nothing and might achieve more than trying to run. She was a good sprinter but her haversack would slow her down and she had no intention of parting with it; for one thing, it held the only money she had in the world. Moreover, she knew that flight often triggered pursuit. Ignoring the spurious endearment, "Hullo," she said brightly. "Are you going near the bus station? Perhaps you wouldn't mind seeing me there?"

"We can see you here." All four sniggered at the witticism.

"I meant see that I get there safely."

"We know what you meant," said the leader. "We'll see that you get there safely. But first, you can do us a favour before we do you one? Right, lads?" There was a mutter of agreement.

"What sort of favour?" Polly asked in as firm a voice as she could manage. It was, she knew, a silly question. She had had at least a theoretical grounding in what the school had called The Facts of Life and one of her teachers had been tediously explicit about the desires of the young male.

The reply came in deeds, not words. These were not experienced rapists – the sudden appearance of an easy target had broken the restraint imposed by fear of the consequences and each was now feeding on the momentum of his companions. If one of them had turned chicken, the others might have been relieved to let her go, but they would never have let him forget his humiliation.

They laid hands on her, clumsily. Polly was a healthy young woman, made more so by years of compulsory school games and sports, and she fought with grim determination. There was a hand over her mouth. She tried and failed to bite but the hand was jerked away and she uttered a scream. She nearly broke loose but one of the youths, stronger or more determined than the others, managed to twist her arms behind her, where they tangled with the straps of her haversack. She was dragged towards a nearby gateway. She kicked and lost a shoe. Another of the boys was already fumbling at her clothes. She screamed again, but it seemed to be an area of businesses and not a residential neighbourhood.

Just as she was wondering whether graceful submission might not save her from an even worse fate, another figure loomed in front of her, coming out of nowhere, heavier than the others and more ominous in what looked like black leather. She aimed a kick at it but the figure side-stepped easily. "Naughty, naughty," it said.

A second later, it became clear that the reproof was not addressed to Polly and that this was not another assailant come to join the fun but was the modern equivalent of the US cavalry or a knight in shining armour galumphing to the rescue. Two heads came together with a clunk which in retrospect made Polly feel sick, and two of the youths fell to the ground. A third, the one who had been interfering with her clothes, made a run for it. The fourth released her arms and would have followed but was grabbed by her rescuer and held clear of the ground in a waist-hold which clearly kept him unable to breathe.

"Are you all right, Miss?" the newcomer asked her.

Polly was short of breath, her knees were loose, her mouth was very dry and she suspected that her arms would have stiffened by the next day. She felt anything but all right but was too proud to say so. "I think so," she said.

Then man addressed his captive. "Then I'm going to turn you loose," he said. "But first I'm going to give you something to hand on to your pal. You understand me?" The youth, whose eyes were beginning to pop, made a strangled sound. "You understand?" the rescuer said again, increasing pressure.

The youth began a frantic nodding. "Good. Here's what I want you to pass along. Tell him to remember it. It's just this. Next time you fancy giving a girl a hard time I may be standing just behind you, making ready to do this."

Polly averted her eyes while the youth, restored to his feet, underwent an experience which, to judge from the sounds that he managed to make with his returning breath, was beyond bearing. "You'll remember?"

"I'll remember, I'll remember," gabbled the youth.

"You'll pass it on?"

"You can bet on it."

"Good. Here's a spare one in case you forget." Polly looked away again. She spotted her shoe lying near the gutter and limped across to put it on. The sounds went on for longer this time. "Now, bugger off."

The youth did as he was bid, without dallying.

"We better beat it," the man in black leather said

dispassionately. "Some berk's probably called the fuzz by now and if I've damaged one of these yobs there may be trouble." Two of the attackers were still on the ground but each seemed to be moving. He stirred them with his foot and then turned away. "Come on. It's time you were somewhere else." He avoided looking at her. She thought that he was trying to avoid embarrassing her.

Rather than be alone again in this hostile environment, Polly followed him to a large motorcycle which seemed to have materialised beside the kerb. "Hop up," he said. "Where were you going?"

"The bus station."

"There'll be nobody there, this time of night." He straddled the bike, paused and looked into her face and away again. In the aftermath of her adventure, Polly wanted to cry. She wanted to be at home in her bed under the eaves. She wanted to be somewhere safe. She wanted someone else to take decision-making out of her hands, just for the moment. "Hey, you need a drink. Hop up," he said again.

Polly climbed up onto a surprisingly comfortable pillion. She had a feeling that she was showing more leg than was proper but she refused to look down. The man twisted in the saddle and put a large crash helmet over her curls, giving it a reassuring tap. He remained bare-headed. There was no need for so mundane an act as kick-starting; at the touch of a button the engine turned over and the handsome machine began to throb and then moved away with a suggestion of effortless power. Polly clung for dear life to the black leather and exulted in the motion, in safety, in danger, in escape from everybody and everything. The long street was no longer menacing. The world could not get at her now.

They passed the railway station, crossed a broad square which Polly recognised from her occasional visits to the city with an earlier 'uncle', climbed a hill, skirted a small park and entered a road of tall Victorian terraced houses built of stone and with bay windows running their full height. At street level, deep basements were protected by iron railings. Cars were parked on both sides but there was still ample room for traffic. In a tiny garden on the corner, a willow was beginning to shed its leaves.

The bike came to a halt outside the first of the houses. The man turned in the saddle. "You hop down here," he said. "You'll be quite safe and anyway you won't be out of my sight for more than a second or two. I'll be right back."

By now, Polly would have trusted him with her life. She got down. In her relief, she had savoured the ride despite the cold. But she was not dressed for motor-cycling at midnight in autumn and she felt herself beginning to shiver. The machine moved away. Suddenly it swerved across the street, as if the rider had suffered a stroke. Polly watched, surprised but accepting the unusual as having become the norm, as he rode the bike straight up a flight of steps, halted for no more than a second at the top as he leaned forward to insert a key in the door, and then rode his bike straight into the house.

The promised 'second or two' stretched to nearly a minute, but even when a basement door close to where she was standing suddenly spilled light and two men came up the steps, Polly felt quite safe. The men glanced at her and one of them hesitated, but they walked away.

Her rescuer returned. He had stripped off his leathers and by the lamp above the nearest door she saw that he

13

was wearing twill trousers and a Fair Isle sweater over a checked shirt. She was able to take him in for the first time. In the excitement of the rescue she had seen him through rose-coloured and magnifying spectacles. She now saw that, instead of being eight feet tall, he was only an inch or two taller than herself and although his features were pleasant enough in a square-jawed, blunt-nosed way, only a fond mother would have considered him handsome. He was thickset, obviously muscular, and he moved with a confident grace. Tight blond curls triggered an indistinct memory.

"I've seen you somewhere before," she said. "Or somebody very like you."

"Oh yes?"

"On television, I think. Are you an actor?"

'Sort of. We're all actors in one way or another. Come on inside before you freeze your little bum off." She had seen him, she was sure of it, yet she had never heard his voice before.

He led her into a large room fitted out much like the cocktail bar in a hotel which Polly's mother had frequented during one of her more affluent periods. Money had been spent. The seats were covered in what looked like real hide, the wallpaper was one that Polly recognised from the pattern books as costing a fortune an inch, the carpet was deep and soft and, although the décor was slightly Victorian, the ceiling was finished with acoustic tiles which damped out the voices of a small group of men who were huddled in a corner. Otherwise, they had the room to themselves. Her companion deposited her in a chair in the diametrically opposite corner to the men and went to a well-fitted and well-stocked bar, presided over by a dignified lady in black velvet who was exhibiting a quite remarkable cleavage. He came back carrying a pint glass of what she supposed was probably beer and a smaller glass holding an inch of some amber liquid. He set the smaller glass in front of her and sat down opposite.

Polly had been looking around while considering his remark about actors. The arrival of the strange drink brought her back to the here and now. "What's this?" she asked, in curiosity rather than suspicion.

"A small brandy. You'll need it, after being set on like that and then going pillion in the cold. This one's on me." The significance of this last remark only dawned on her later.

In a day so filled with strange events, a first acquaintance with brandy was only to be expected. She took a tiny sip. It was strong yet comforting but she decided that she would never develop a taste for it. She thanked him. "Is this a nightclub?" she asked.

"Kind of," he said. "It's a gaming club. The upper floors and the big room at the back are mostly for gambling. I don't go in for much of that. It's a mug's game. If you gamble because you need the money, sure as hell you'll lose. But if you go with just as much money as you don't mind losing, that's okay if it's what turns you on and you may stand a chance of winning, even. I stay a member because I'm often on the way home at this time of night and I may feel the need of a pint, but I won't take one until I've finished riding the bike. I'd be lost without my license. Now tell me about you."

"Me?"

He had a friendly smile which, she decided, improved his looks dramatically, but he was still hesitant about making eye-contact with her. "Yes, you. I find you being mauled by a bunch of scruffs. You say you're going to the bus station, which wouldn't be open at this time of night. So I give you a lift here and you don't ask to be taken somewhere else or seem to give a damn where you go. I hope you don't think you're going to crawl into my bed. So what do you want? Shall I put you in a taxi, or what?"

Put like that, Polly could see that her circumstances did need a little explaining. More to the point, she realised that she was now running out of options. It took only a little more coaxing before she began to tell her whole story. On only one facet was she less than frank. She was still a few days short of her eighteenth birthday but she had matured in face and figure over the preceding year. She could, she knew, pass for older than her seventeen years, so she added a little to her age. Even so, her companion tutted and looked a little guilty when she proclaimed herself as eighteen. She gathered that even eighteen was not really senior enough for these premises.

When she came to a halt, her companion was shaking his head. "You don't want to go to London," he said, unconsciously echoing the van driver. "What little money you've got would be gone in a day, and then what? You'd be living in a cardboard box, same as thousands of others. And what after that? If drugs didn't get you, AIDS would. You'd do better to stick around here."

She felt a shiver run up her back. "This isn't a trap, is it? You're not going to contact my mother?"

He looked at her as though she had gone mad. "How would I know your mother from Eve? Anyway, you're eighteen. There's nothing she could do about it."

"And you think that I'd be better sleeping in a cardboard box nearer home?"

"I think you've more chance of a job and a life here than in the Smoke. Anyway, you can do what the hell you like in the morning. For the moment, you'd better come back with me. I can lend you a bed for what's left of the night."

Polly looked at him sharply. Until then, her best guess had been that, having saved her from one fate, he felt obliged to see her all the way out of trouble. His conduct so far had not suggested such a thing, but this might be the point at which he expected his reward for saving her from a much rougher experience. If so . . . Several of her friends had discarded their virginities at much the same age and, provided the sacrifice was made with care and discretion, had not regretted the loss. On the other hand Polly, though well grounded in the theory of sex, had no desire for the gritty mechanism of it in connection with herself. In a mind becoming slightly fuddled by the unaccustomed brandy, she wondered whether there had really been an obligation on the recently rescued maiden to repay the rescuing knight in a manner that might well leave her in more distress than before his arrival . . .

Her companion guessed the direction of her thoughts. He half smiled. "You don't have to worry about me," he said. "I . . . don't love girls."

The sentiment was so close to one expressed by most of the boys of her acquaintance up to the age of puberty that Polly nearly took the statement at face value. Then she remembered that one or two of those boys, from shyness or inclination, had carried that rejection of her sex into adult life. "You're—" she was on the point of choosing between *homosexual*

17

and *gay*, but decided to avoid any risk of hurting his feelings, substituted, "—sure?"

He nodded. "Quite sure. I own that house, the one where I took the bike. I let the rooms off. That's what you might call my pension fund. The girl who has the first floor back, she's moving out, going to live with her boyfriend. A bad move, in my opinion. He's a louse. Hugo Something, an airline steward. I was going to give her the push anyway and she knew it, so maybe that made up her mind for her. She won't be sleeping there anymore. You can have her room for the night, free of charge because she's paid up for the rest of the week."

"That's very kind of you," Polly said politely.

He waved the courtesy aside. "Not kind at all. You tell me that you've no plans and nowhere to go. Fair enough. I've been placed the same way before now. But it could be that we can help each other out. I'm half hoping that you'll take the room over. You'd be a lot less trouble, that's for sure. Diana – the other girl – works in a massage parlour. Next thing to being a tart. I could turn a blind eye to that, as long as she didn't bring them home. But I'm pretty sure she's started sniffing coke. That could bring all sorts of trouble, cops in the night and all that. She had to go. I've started looking out for somebody reliable, somebody I can be sure wouldn't be trouble."

"You think I wouldn't be trouble?"

He met her eyes for the first time, then smiled. "You could be trouble, all right, but not that sort of trouble."

Polly felt suitably flattered. She stole another look at the man. A bruise was developing below his left eye. "Did one of those toughs manage to mark you?" she asked him.

He touched his face and then shook his head contemptuously. "It'd take more than that lot."

The four men in the far corner seemed to have finished what had become an argument. They finished their drinks and made for the door. One of them, the biggest, turned aside and loomed over them. His features were harsh almost to the point of caricature and he had what Polly thought of as designer stubble. "You've thought about it?" he demanded.

"I've thought about it," said Polly's rescuer.

"And?"

"And I've told you before, over and over, I don't want any part of anything."

"Think some more. You're tough but you're not immortal." He turned without another word and lumbered towards the door.

"Who on earth was that?" Polly asked.

"That was Ronald Dent. Anything bad happens around here, it's six to four that he's at the back of it, or maybe out in front. If you stick around here, that's one person to steer miles clear of. Because I travel around a lot and, like he said, I'm tough, he wants me to carry stuff around for him."

"What sort of stuff?"

"I've never asked and I'd rather not guess. But what I do guess is that either Dent or Hugo, the boyfriend, is supplying Diana and she'll find herself doing the horizontal tango with all comers just to pay for her supplies if she doesn't kick it bloody quick. And I've told her so. But she's a silly cow and she won't listen to good advice. But then, who does?"

19

Polly's earlier life, which had sometimes seemed distinctly seamy, looked in retrospect as dull and respectable as a vicarage tea-party. Whole new perspectives were opening up around her. But an unexpected recollection distracted her. "You're a wrestler," she said suddenly. "I've seen you."

"On the telly?"

"And live." One of Polly's 'uncles' had been a devoted follower and had often taken her with him to matinée events. "You're Darryl Davidson. Right?"

"Can't hide from you. And I'm the Masked Marauder as well."

Polly was shocked. "But he's one of the bad guys!"

Darryl Davidson laughed aloud, bringing to his face the good looks that it lacked in repose. "You only have to let the crowd see you break the rules on the ref's blind side and they'll believe you're the devil in a leotard. Then they'll come in droves and pay good money in the hope of seeing you get flattened. Then your fees go up. Matter of fact, I only took the name over from another wrestler when he retired."

"You look bigger in the ring."

"One does. Some of them are real short-arses."

It had been a long day and Polly had disposed of her brandy. She was becoming very sleepy again, but one more revelation came to her. "That's why you wanted to get away from that place quickly."

"That's it. The beaks don't take kindly to a professional fighter who duffs up some member of the public, and never mind the provocation. You can get six months for defending yourself." He finished the last of his pint. "And now, young Polly, Madge is waiting to close up and it's high time you were in bed. Come with me."

Polly retrieved her haversack from behind her chair and followed him out into the faint signs of dawn.

Two

Drugged with brandy and exhaustion, Polly was hardly aware of going to bed, but she woke suddenly and completely to hunger, sunshine, the sounds of traffic and what was obviously the middle of other people's day. It took her some seconds to recall where she was, and why. Then she felt a smile spread over her whole body. Her doubts were gone with the darkness. It was a new day, a new city, a new life. The bed smelt, not unpleasantly, of the oils and unguents used by the absent Diana.

Darryl Davidson, she seemed to recall, had mentioned the existence of two communal bathrooms, but the room was equipped with a sink as well as a tiny cooker. A saucepan and a few items of cutlery and crockery, enough for one person, stood forlornly on the draining board. The room, as was to be expected for its period, was spacious. It had been decorated unimaginatively in pale green but somebody, presumably Diana, had tried to apply a feminine touch by adding pink frills around the window and a matching fringe round the bed. The result, Polly thought, was hideous. The furniture was sturdy, upholstered in another green and from the middle price range, possibly second-hand but in good condition. The cupboards were empty – even, to her disappointment, the small fridge and the food cupboard under the draining board. Several cardboard cartons were filled with the other woman's possessions, awaiting collection. The clothes had been packed with some care and then the toiletries and odds and ends tumbled in on top. Polly's first act to impress her own personality on the room was to remove the pink frills and fold them carefully into the cartons.

Polly washed at the sink and then got dressed in what she considered to be her only adult ensemble of skirt (too long) and jumper (not matching the skirt and in a hideous colour favoured by the school before last). She brushed her hair into a style which she thought made her look at least twenty and rather prim.

Only when she was as satisfied as she could be with her image did she turn away from the mirror and think to look out of the window. She was pleased to find that the ground fell away and that she was looking through a screen of mature trees and over a few rooftops to open farmland, several woods and, in the distance, the gleam of water. The view through the trees was opening up as the leaves fell, so that she could see a tractor ploughing stubble and some sheep hurrying aimlessly from one corner of a field to another. Polly had lived most of her life in the country. Living in a city would be constricting, but less so with such an outlook to come back to.

She was on the point of venturing out in search of, first, the nearest bathroom and then a late breakfast, when there was a knock at the door and she found Darryl Davidson on the landing. He was dressed in an old tracksuit and trainers. "Diana won't have left any food for you," he said. "Lock your door and come down and I'll give you a cup of tea and a slice of toast."

His tone was self-congratulatory. Later, she realised that, driven by a fear of penury in the early retirement faced by wrestlers, he was excessively careful with money. He could be generous with his time or with help and he would spend money, very carefully, for his own amenities, but that was the limit of his extravagance.

Gratefully, Polly dropped the latch on her door and followed him down the stairs into a large sized hall in which stood, isolated on their own plastic matting above the Wilton carpet and looking rather like sculptures at an exhibition of very modern art, the motorcycle from the previous night and a much older Lambretta scooter. They gave the bare hallway a look of purpose. He led her into an apartment which seemed to occupy most of the ground floor. The sitting-dining-kitchen was brightly decorated by a skilled but less than professional hand and more comfortably furnished than the room above. He pointed out a chair at a small dining table, poured her a mug of tea and set a toaster to work.

"Whose is the scooter?" she asked. It might have been evidence of somebody closer to her own age about the place.

"They're both mine," he said. "I use the scooter around the town. It's cheap to run and, some places I go, you don't leave a top-of-the-range bike on the street and expect to find all of it there when you come back. An old scooter doesn't invite envy, so they leave it alone, mostly, or if they pinch bits off it they don't cost much to replace. When I have time, I run. Are you any good at gardening?"

The abrupt change of subject made her blink, but, "I'm real good," she said. It was the truth. The 'uncle' who had preceded the wrestling fan had been a passionate gardener with the knack of communicating both knowledge and enthusiasm and, ever since, she had undertaken such gardening as was called for wherever they happened to be living at the time.

"That's to the good," he said. "I like the place well kept, it's good for values. Diana did the gardening. She hated it and did it badly, but I made it a condition of her having the room. My other tenants are old or handicapped, except for an Asian lady who doesn't understand our plants and the man in the top floor back. He keeps the room as a love-nest and he's only here once in a blue moon when his luck's in. I'm usually too busy to look at the garden and the green on my fingers is arsenic. If you take on the garden I can let you have the room, electricity included . . ." he studied her musingly and then stated a rent. This seemed to Polly to be a lot of money, but the nest-egg in the bottom of her haversack would be enough for the first few weeks, by which time she would surely have found a job or been found and forced to return home. Perhaps her mother would have quarrelled with the latest one. He had already lasted longer than most.

They shook hands on the deal. "You're going to stay, then," Darryl said with satisfaction.

"At least until I've run out of clean laundry."

He looked hurt. "I have a washing machine," he said quickly. "Use it whenever you like."

"I was joking," Polly explained. She set about her toast and marmalade with relish but made a mental note to buy in a few essentials such as cereals and eggs. For all her careful dietary habits, she was used to a good country breakfast.

"Great!" Darryl said. "Today or tomorrow I'll want

two weeks rent in advance. I can give you a key to the front door now. I'll have to get Diana's room key off her when she comes for her things. For the moment, I'll use my master-key to let you back into your room. After that, until I've caught up with the silly bitch, you'll just have to leave it open or catch me again. I'll be in and out most of the day."

Polly, her mouth full, just nodded.

Back in her room, she recovered the small hoard from her haversack. What remained was hardly worth stealing. She left the room unlocked.

Before leaving for the shops, she found the back door and studied the garden. Diana, it seemed, had been a less than adventurous gardener, confining her efforts to cutting the grass and occasionally hoeing between the few established shrubs. But there was a small greenhouse in reasonable condition and there she found flowerpots and even a sack of peat. A shed built onto the back of the house held a formidable lawnmower and some rusty garden tools. Among the useless odds and ends on a small bench she found an adjustable spanner and an oil can.

Polly walked to the shops which they had passed the previous night, a row catering to local custom, now open and bustling with customers of many races. She spent a pleasant hour browsing, comparing prices and eventually making thrifty purchases of basic necessities of food and toiletries. A hardware store furnished her with a cheap kettle and some other essentials.

Back at the house she put away her purchases, stowed the remains of her money in the toe of a shoe in the very bottom of her haversack and changed into trainers, jeans

27

and a thin sweater. The morning had almost gone. She made and ate a cheese salad and dropped the lock on the door of the room before going back to the garden.

The grass was dry but the mower, which was powered only by human sweat, was an ungainly beast and in poor condition. Polly had met such creatures before and tamed them. Ten minutes with the oil can and a spanner had the mower taking a shallow cut with no more effort required than would be needed to push-start a small lorry. In a further hour, the lawn was mown and the cut grass, mixed with strips of newspaper from below the stairs, deposited on a long forgotten compost heap. The day was cold but she had worked up a sweat. That, she decided, was enough heavy work for the moment. There were plenty of flowerpots in the greenhouse and Polly set about taking cuttings of the more worthwhile shrubs and perennials using rooting compound which she had brought from the hardware store, and enclosing the pots of cuttings in polythene bags thriftily saved from her purchases. It was a little late in the year for taking cuttings, but well worth the attempt.

Polly looked around the garden once more. Already, it looked happier, as if it knew that somebody cared. She would have liked to fork over the barren areas, trim the edges of the grass and make a start on rebuilding an old rockery and dry stone retaining wall which had never, in Polly's opinion, been well designed and had begun to disintegrate. But much more of the day had gone by than she'd realised and she suddenly discovered that, in addition to being satisfied for the moment, she was also tired and hungry.

In the hallway, she found Darryl in the act of parking the Lambretta beside its big brother.

"Will you let me into my room, please?" she asked.

"Here's your key." He held it out to her. "Diana came for her boxes and I made sure I got it off her. Do you want an evening job?"

"I'll have to get some sort of a job," she said. "I've been wondering what to do about it."

"I can see you've got a problem," he said. "No cards, no NI number, no nothing. But if you want a casual cleaner's job, I can fix you up. Strictly cash, daily basis, and if you fall ill I've never heard of you."

"That's the sort of thing I was hoping for."

"Come along then. We'll take the scooter."

"Give me a minute to change and have a shower. I'm all sweaty."

"You'll be worse before you're better."

"At least give me a moment to eat. I haven't had anything since an early lunch and I didn't exactly gorge myself then."

"There's a good chippy next door to where we're going."

The world seemed to be conspiring to sweep away her good habits. "I haven't got any money on me."

That turned out to be a more convincing argument. He paused. "I'll advance you something against your first day's pay," he said at last. "Come on."

So Polly found herself being swept through the streets again, this time on the back of a noisy, popping little scooter. They went a bare half-mile, turned off into a side street and then into a yard and stopped in front of what seemed to have originated as a warehouse. The word GYMNASIUM was painted, not perfectly straight, across the front.

* * *

On the street corner, a fish and chip emporium had opened for business only half an hour earlier. While they waited for the first batch of chips to turn a suitably autumnal brown, Darryl explained. "That's my gym. I don't mean that I just use it, though I do, a lot. But it used to be owned and run by an old boxer. When the hammerings he'd taken over the years got to him and he had to retire, I borrowed the money and bought the place. It's my second pension fund. Gladys, my daily cleaner, just left her husband and went off to Spain with a circus acrobat who came here to loosen up after a fall."

"Another bad move, you think?" Polly asked idly.

"Quite a good one. Her husband's a louse. And she's always had a fondness for acrobats. They make good lovers, she says." He paused. "You're not shocked?" he asked her.

"Not a bit. I'll have to remember her advice," Polly said. "And the gymnasium is where I'm to clean?"

"If you want the job. You won't meet many toffs. There's several much more up-market health clubs where the businessmen go to play squash, get rid of their hangovers and shake off a few kilos under doctor's supervision, but this is where boxers, wrestlers and a lot of the athletes come to sweat it off. And then they come in here and put it all on again."

"And bloody good thing too," said the proprietor, an enormously fat man with a trace of Italian accent. "Otherwise I soon starve." The meal was ready and he served Polly's plaice and chips in a neat polystyrene box.

"Which would do you a whole lot of good, Fatso," Darryl said amiably. "You want to come next door and work out, now and again. And again." He handed Polly a five pound note. She paid for her meal and returned the change.

They walked back to the door of the gym. Darryl looked up at the sky. "Be dark soon," he said. "Hold the door for me." He wheeled the scooter into a large, warm and brightly lit space where sounds of exertion echoed to and fro. The decor was spartan: bare brickwork had been painted an institutional cream. Above, the latticework of steel trusses was threaded with old ductwork, most of it obviously disused and hung with cobwebs. In the middle of the floorspace, two boxers were sparring in a ring, urged on by a trainer and several bystanders. On a mat, another two were locked in painful looking wrestling holds. Other men, in trunks or leotards, were busy exercising on equipment and at machines. The predominant smell was of embrocation and sweat.

Darryl raised his voice. "Hoy!" he shouted. There was comparative silence except when one of the boxers dropped his guard and his sparring partner floored him. "Mind your language. There's a lady present. This is Polly, everyone. She'll be around for a while."

A large man who had been performing very creditably with a skipping rope came over, a friendly grin on his battered face. "Hi, Polly," he said and put out a hand. Polly was about to shake it when he helped himself to one of her chips and turned away. Polly shrugged. He was more likely to work off the extra few grams of fat than she was.

The void had looked as large as an aircraft hanger. Polly now saw that it was only as big as a medium-sized supermarket, but big for all that. "I'm not supposed to scrub the whole of this place, am I?" she asked.

31

Darryl shook his head. "Four ladies come in on
Sundays to scrub right through," he said. "But you
do what Gladys used to do. You sweep this room
and give the changing room and showers a good
wash with disinfectant. We don't want any exchanges
of foot-fungus around here. And I'll want you to lock up
for me when I'm away. I'll show you where everything is,
after we close. At ten, usually, but we're flexible."

"Shall I come back at ten?"

"Hang about. There's always somebody wants an
errand run."

So Polly hung about, keeping well clear of the changing
rooms and showers. She ran errands to the shops or the
pub – a sandwich, a diet coke, talcum or some sticking
plaster. She placed bets at a betting shop half a street
away and once collected some winnings. There was a
small laundry room behind the office and several men
left sweaty clothes in the washing machines and slipped
Polly a *pourboire* to take them out when finished, put
them through the tumble drier and leave them on a
hook for next day. Her gardening clothes seemed quite
appropriate for the place and the company. She adopted
a trace of the local, rural accent that she had learned to
hide behind when lack of funds forced her transfer to
one village school or another. Between times, she sat
in the cramped office where Darryl was attending to
paperwork between bouts of working out. Most of the
men, she learned, paid a regular subscription plus a small
fee for each attendance. Others, non-members, paid only
a stiffer attendance fee. There were those who could not
be trusted to fill in the honesty book and several times
Polly was sent to count heads.

When the last members departed, Polly was already at

work with an over-width broom. Darryl showered. Then, while he finished his ledgers, she took a mop and bucket and some pungent disinfectant, collected forgotten odds and ends – including a denture – for the Lost and Found cupboard and blitzed the changing room and showers. While she worked, she could feel the weight of coins in the pocket of her jeans. She had never been so rich. A lucky gambler had been particularly generous.

It was not far off midnight and the streets were beginning to sleep when Darryl locked up carefully and kicked the scooter into life. Polly hopped up behind and they puttered back through the empty dark. When the scooter was safely up the steps, Darryl peeled a note off a roll held by a rubber band and handed it over. His expression was meant to be friendly or even avuncular, but he looked pained.

Polly, who was beginning to understand him, decided to cheer him up. She had already counted her tips but the total in her pocket still fell short of what she needed. "If you come upstairs for a moment," she said, "I'll give you your two weeks rent."

Darryl cheered up.

But, upstairs, she found that her haversack seemed to be packed less systematically than when she had left it and no amount of fumbling could produce her mother's alligator purse. With a hollow sense of foreboding, she dumped everything out on the bed but there could be no doubt about it.

"I've been robbed," she said desolately.

"You don't mean it!"

"I'm not joking," Polly said. "My money's gone."

Darryl opened and closed his mouth several times, uncertain what to say. "Tomorrow will do," he said

33

at last. "No hurry." He turned to the door. "Good-night."

"Wait!" The sharpness in Polly's voice jerked him to a halt. "I should think tomorrow bloody well would do! Where did that Diana move to?"

"How much money was it?" When she told him, he said, "Peanuts! You can make that in less than a week. Forget it. Write it off to experience."

"What do you mean?"

He shrugged. "Let it teach you something. Don't let it happen to you again."

Polly grabbed for the departing shreds of her temper. "I didn't let it happen to me at all. *You* let it happen to me. You opened my door and left her in here alone."

He had the grace not to argue. "Look," he said, "I can't get involved in disputes."

"Because the courts are hard on professional fighters who engage in fights outside the ring. I understand that."

"And you forgive me?"

"No, I don't bloody well forgive you," Polly snapped. "You were responsible and you know it and if I can't get my money back I'll expect you to make good the loss. But all I'm asking you for the moment is where she moved to. And a loan of the scooter."

"You can ride a scooter?"

"Certainly." This was true. A schoolfriend had taught her on farm roads and byways. There was no need to mention her lack of a driving license. She had thrown off parental and school discipline and the whole ethical code of her childhood, so it seemed that laws also no longer applied to her. From now on, she would live by the eleventh commandment, *Thou shalt not be found out.*

"If the boyfriend's there. . . ." Darryl began.

"I'll come away, I promise. But you said that he was an airline steward? He could be in Australia."

"Well, all right," Darryl said reluctantly.

As she rode the scooter through the streets, fumbling with unfamiliar gears and following from memory the sketch map that Darryl had drawn for her, Polly's mind was filled with conflicting emotions. On the one hand, Darryl had been right. The sum *was* comparatively small. But it represented security of a sort. It was hers, to set her on the track to independence. Nobody was going to find her a soft target. If that happened once it might happen again, because she would have accepted the role of victim.

The address turned out to be a tenement flat in a large block crammed in between prim little semi-detached houses. The front door of the block was open. Polly climbed two stairs and found a door bearing a card which read 'Hugo Tyrone'.

She stopped to think some more. It was the middle of the night. If she rang the bell and admitted her identity, her chances of being allowed inside were nil. She could claim to be something official, but could not see herself sustaining such a role. Her mother's purse, when she purloined it, had contained a credit card which she had transferred, for no very good reason, to the pocket of her anorak. Fiction had it that a spring lock could be slipped with a credit card. After some thought, she decided to test the relationship between fiction and fact. And if Diana's Tyrone happened to be present she would have more time to run for it and ride furiously into the distance.

The use of the credit card was not the simple matter

that she had been allowed to assume, especially when she needed to work in silence for fear of ambush. Every sound was loud in the night-silent building. By the time the lock gave way with a soft click she doubted whether the card would ever be usable again, but she had no intention of fraudulently using her mother's card anyway. Apart from the endless complications which could follow, she had no wish to remain a burden, at whatever range, on her mother. Besides, the card had probably been cancelled by now.

She could hear the faint sounds of at least one sleeper. She reached to the wall inside the dark room, found a light switch and, uttering a silent prayer, pressed it down.

The untidy room was suddenly bright. In an extended bed-settee, one person slept. From the hair flowing over the pillow, Polly guessed that the sleeper was a woman. Even by today's standards, long hair dyed unnaturally blonde would probably not be favoured on airline stewards. She stepped inside and pulled the door shut behind her.

The sleeper roused, rolled over and put up a hand to keep the light out of her eyes. "Don't bugger about," she said. "Come to bed."

Polly ignored the invitation. She had a few seconds for undisturbed study of the room but before she could settle on the most likely place for her money the other woman – Diana – sat up suddenly. "Who the hell are you?" she demanded shrilly.

"I'm the person you robbed," Polly replied.

"Who?"

"How many have there been?"

During this short exchange, Polly had been looking

around the room. There was a discernible logic in the chaos. Discarded clothing had been left where it fell, but clean clothes, mostly recent purchases, had been deposited wherever a flat surface had been available. A remarkable collection of cosmetics of every sort and shade filled any remaining gaps. But Polly spotted an imitation leather handbag half hidden by a pair of tights in the seat of a worn fireside chair. She made for it.

The sleeper was now fully awake and had no intention of giving up her loot. With remarkable agility, considering that she had been deeply asleep a few seconds earlier, she catapulted out of bed and got between Polly and the chair. She had been sleeping nude.

"No you bloody don't," she said. She put her hands on Polly's shoulders and began to push her towards the door.

Polly pushed her away. Diana stumbled back. She was older than Polly – almost twice her age, Polly thought – and her generous breasts, which seemed to be succumbing to time and the force of gravity, described remarkable figures in the air. She lost her temper and came at Polly again, aiming for Polly's face with her fingernails.

That was a mistake. Diana had developed muscles during her career as a masseuse, but Polly was young and she had been the terror of the hockey and lacrosse fields. Moreover, in the course of frequent changes of school, up and down the market as her mother's fortunes had waxed and waned, she had had to learn to defend herself against bullies of both sexes. She had learned to fight like a boy. She had also learned never to fight at all without going all out for a quick win. She ducked her head. Diana's first, wild attack knocked off her crash helmet. The other's fingers closed in her hair. Polly punched the other girl hard in the stomach, just below the breast-bone.

The move was not quite as painless to Polly as she had hoped. Diana began to fold without immediately releasing her hair. Polly was forced to bend double. Then the grip was released and Diana sat down hard and changed colour. She rolled up into a foetal position.

Relieved of this distraction, Polly picked up the imitation leather bag. It proved to be full almost to overflowing, with tissues both clean and used, a spare set of tights, dozens of receipts and credit card slips and more items of cosmetics than Polly would have believed existed. The inside of the bag being black, it took her some seconds to find her mother's alligator purse in an internal pocket. She looked inside to be sure that there was money there. Her eyes were watering from the tug at her hair but she could make out two ten pound notes, or perhaps both ends of a single note folded. She did not care which. Honour would be satisfied.

Diana's eyes were popping. She was an undignified spectacle. She had rolled onto her back and was kicking her heels in a struggle to find her breath, but she managed to shake her head to and for in a gesture of negativism.

"But yes," Polly said. She dropped the purse into her pocket.

Diana managed to draw a painful breath. "Not yours," she wheezed. She began to struggle up, but when Polly stooped over her she collapsed again. "Some's mine," she added.

"Tough," Polly said. "If it's okay for you to steal from me then it's okay for me to steal from you. Isn't it? What do you think?"

A Running Jump

The other sensibly ignored the trick question. "My boyfriend will have something to say about this," she whispered.

"If he does . . ." Polly began. She was remembering something in the other's handbag, something which had not seemed quite like an item of cosmetics. She picked up the bag again. Out of the corner of her eye she saw a movement. "If you get up, I'll break your fingers," she said. It was a bluff, but a good one. Broken fingers would end the career of a masseuse.

"You wouldn't!"

Polly looked her in the eye. "You stole every penny I had in the world. If you really think I wouldn't, try getting up."

Diana subsided again.

Polly found what she had been looking for. It was a small and unlabelled brown plastic bottle, as used for the dispensing of medicines, but it contained a quantity of powder quite unsuited to the bottle. "If I ever hear from you or your miserable boyfriend again," she said, "I'll tell the police that he's supplying you with drugs and that they can confirm that drugs are present here by testing your carpet and – and things."

Diana uttered a moan of protest but never moved as Polly uncapped the bottle and dusted the powder over the carpet and the furniture.

"Not all of it," Diana whispered. "Leave a little."

"I'll leave you as much as you left me." She spilled the last of it onto the bare floorboards around the edge of the room. Even if the couple replaced all their furnishings, there would still be traces in the joints between the floorboards. "You can get up now, if you like," she said. She left the room, slamming the door.

Three

Polly was becoming almost accustomed to the life of a night-bird but she found, when she had stowed the scooter back in Darryl's hall, that despite her earlier surge of adrenalin she was ready to yawn her head off. She took herself off to bed. She slept with the window open but her room faced away from the traffic and she could have slept through a rock concert. She slept the sleep of the young and exhausted, once again waking, fully rested and content, only when life outside was already in full swing.

Then, over a light breakfast in her own room, she looked in her mother's purse for the first time and, with mixed emotions, discovered that she had made a substantial profit on the night's work. Smaller notes might have vanished, but in their place were several notes of a denomination such as Polly had never set eyes on before. At a rough count, she had made off with more than four hundred pounds of Diana's money. There was also a slip of paper, which she ignored.

Her first impulse was to return the surplus money. But there came back to her the argument which she had put to Diana. What was sauce for the goose was sauce for the gander and tit was definitely for tat. The fact that the earnings had probably been immoral, she decided, was irrelevant. Most money had passed through illicit hands at some time or another.

But her mother, having once been burgled, had always set her face against having too much money in the house. Added to her earnings of the previous night, and in view of the previous day's experience, this undoubtedly came within the 'too much' bracket. She had intended to spend the morning in the garden, forking over the bare areas between the shrubs, but she was a girl with an inadequate wardrobe and money to spend. She made herself as tidy and respectable as she could manage. She tied her hair back, which she was sure lent her appearance an air of maturity and responsibility.

She caught Darryl as he prepared to leave for his morning's workout in the empty gym, gave him a very brief résumé of the night's events and paid him his two weeks advance rent. (Darryl quite agreed that she had a moral if not a legal right to the money.) Then she set off for the shops. A golden autumn sunshine lent the severe streets an unaccustomed homeliness and there was a new spring in her step.

This was not an occasion for little local shops. She caught a bus to the city centre and found herself among broad streets which were filled with a not unhappy mixture of old buildings and modern.

First she visited a bank, making sure that it was not a branch of any bank where her mother had an account. Armed with her mother's driving license as proof of identity and with a satisfactory story about a move to the city, she had no difficulty opening an account, depositing the surplus money and receiving a cheque book. She and her mother were both 'Pauline' and she had used the surname Turnbull during her mother's second marriage, so a suitable signature came easily. Her personalised cheque book and bank card would arrive in due course, the teller explained, but she was provided with a letter promising the honouring of her cheques up to the balance of the account. If the teller bothered to decode the date of birth coded into the last six figures of the license number, he made no comment.

The lure of the garden still called her, but so did the shops. For a girl with an unused cheque book and, in her opinion, a juvenile wardrobe, the decision was inevitable. She visited a large department store, spending with care and restraint. She bought several pairs of tights, one trouser suit which she was sure would intensify the image of respectability for which she was aiming and, grudgingly, shoes to match. She stocked up with toiletries and carefully chosen makeup and then visited a hairdressing salon which, due to a cancellation, was able take her immediately for a cut and restyle. The result delighted her. She was sure that she over-tipped but she had no regrets.

The remains of the morning seemed to have departed in a rush. Darryl, who hated to cook for himself, had suggested that she meet him for lunch in a carvery where, for a moderate fixed sum, the diner could choose his own meal and eat as much as he fancied. Polly, a modest eater, had considered this unlikely to be good value for her and had decided to look for a small café, but the acquisition of comparative wealth and a new image had to be celebrated and exhibited to the world. She asked her way to the Coronet Hotel and walked there, slightly unsteady in higher heels than she had ever been permitted to wear in the past.

She found Darryl in the carvery, already established at an otherwise vacant table with a heavily laden plate of chicken, beef and salad. He glowed with rude health after his workout and shower. It took him several seconds to recognise Polly. Then he jumped to his feet and pulled out a chair. "By golly!" he said. "You look good enough to eat. Sit down. I'll fetch you something."

Polly was not accustomed to being treated as a real, grown-up lady, nor did such old-world courtesy seem to come naturally to Darryl. Moreover, her frugal soul rebelled at the waste if he should fill her plate on the same scale as his own. "You sit down," she said. "Keep my seat and don't let anyone pinch my bag. I'll go and help myself. You wouldn't know what I'd want anyway."

There was a short queue at the buffet. Polly joined it. She found herself behind a frail, elderly man, a fellow tenant in Darryl's house whom she had met on the landing outside her room. He had introduced himself, very politely, as Mr Shanks.

They chatted guardedly about the weather (which remained fine), Mr Shanks's health (good) and Polly's lovelife (nil). Two places ahead of Mr Shanks and already helping himself she saw a man in a sober suit and tie. His hollow cheeks and slightly protuberant eyes rang a bell with her and she recognised him as having been one of the group in the nightclub with Ronald Dent. He was speaking with animation to a large and horsy-looking lady. His accent was American. "I've seen that man before," she said to make conversation. "Do you know who he is?"

To her surprise, Mr Shanks was a mine of information. "His name's Heindrickson," he said. "I think he's staying in this hotel. He's in the same business as myself –

44

antiques – and he beat me to a nice Sheraton table last week. He's over here on a buying trip. He's in business on his own account, but mostly he acts on behalf of Solomon Meyer in California," Mr Shanks added enviously. "Mr Meyer's mad about Chinese porcelain and can afford to indulge his passion."

"Lucky old him," Polly said.

"Yes indeed. And lucky old Heindrickson."

The queue moved on. Polly paid the set price and helped herself generously to ham, tongue and potato salad. She parted from Mr Shanks, who was lunching with another man, either a colleague or a competitor, and rejoined Darryl. Her meal still looked puny beside his.

"Do I have to find myself another cleaner and gopher?" he asked.

"No. Why should you?"

He waved his fork vaguely. "You don't look that sort of person any more. Have you come into money? Or found a sugar-daddy?"

She laughed. "Neither of those, I'm sorry to say. When I do, I promise you'll be the first to know. I have my old clothes in the carrier-bag. My new hairdo won't suffer if I do a little work. I decided to treat myself to a bit of a makeover with some of Diana's money."

He cheered up. "That's good. You couldn't have put it to a better use. Listen, I've just had a phonecall. Somebody got his arm broken in a practice bout and I've been booked to replace him in Cardiff tonight. I know you've only had one evening's experience, but do you think you could you manage without me?"

"At the gym?"

"Of course at the gym. Slasher usually helps out, but he's not very good at it and I think he lets his friends in

for nothing and still knocks off a little extra for himself.
You'll be all right. They like you and I'll tell somebody
to see you home afterwards."

"What would I have to do?"

"About what you did last night, but make sure any
non-member who comes in pays cash. Members can
put their names in the book. Keep a note of all the
takings and I'll work out the VAT tomorrow. And lock
up afterwards." Darryl paused and thought hard. "You
know what? It's hell having to list all the things you
know so much by heart that you never think about
them. Don't let anybody bring in any alcohol. If you
think one of them's taking drugs, do nothing but tell me
later. I'll deal with it. Slasher will keep you straight."

"I could manage that, I think. Should you be wrestling
on a full stomach?"

Darryl glanced at his digital watch. "About seven
hours? It won't be full by then."

Polly's attention drifted to another subject. She was
not sure which of the wrestlers was known as 'Slasher'
but none of them seemed the type to have earned such
an ominous nickname. If one of them had a criminal
history, she would not want to be associated with him.
"Why do they call him Slasher?" she asked curiously.

"He has an enlarged prostate," Darryl said. "Always
running for a pee. Had to make a dash in the middle of
a bout once and got himself disqualified. What's that
got to do with anything?"

"Not a lot," Polly said.

She accepted a lift to the gym, first inspecting the
scooter to satisfy herself that her new trouser suit would
be in no danger from oil or sharp edges of metal. She
had made up her mind not to indulge in any more

extravagances beyond the cost of survival, but during the journey she decided that one more expenditure would be justified. The way that her new life was shaping up, she would not be spending many evenings in her room; and Darryl, who seemed to have taken her under his wing, had said that she could watch television in his room on Sunday evenings when the gym would be closed. Near the gym, she had noticed a small shop dealing in bargain basement goods, mainly surpluses and remainders, she suspected, or even goods that had fallen off the back of a lorry. She made Darryl let her off outside it. She was looking for a cut-price radio to relieve her mornings in the garden but she settled for a portable stereo and remembered to buy batteries.

Darryl had opened the gym and the first members were already limbering up. Polly earned a few whistles on the way through. The changing rooms were now out of bounds, so she resumed her jeans, sweater and trainers in Darryl's office. That put an end to the whistles. She was relieved and yet slightly disappointed. Male approval might be unnecessary and even sometimes in bad taste, but it did no harm to the ego.

After an hour of fetching and carrying, Darryl called her into the office. "I got to go now," he said. "Slasher will look after you."

"Which one is Slasher?" she asked.

"The big bloke who pinched one of your chips last night. But he can't wait for you to finish cleaning, so I'll leave you the scooter. You ride straight home, remember. No stopping off to get yourself raped. Promise?"

"I promise." Having a friend, and a male friend at that, concerned for her welfare gave her a warm feeling. Her

47

mother's half-concealed anxiety she had found merely irritating.

"And – listen – I've been thinking. Better safe than sorry. That Hugo's a vicious bastard and he won't take kindly to being robbed and threatened – and by a woman."

"He won't want to get the police involved," Polly argued.

"He could move out and let Diana take the rap for the dope. She'd be too scared of him to blow the whistle. So, just for a night or two, we'll swap rooms. Before I leave, I'll put my toothbrush and things in your room. When you get home, you bed down in mine." He put a key into her hand.

"Well, all right," Polly said. "Thanks. If you really think it's necessary."

"I don't know if it's necessary. But I'm damn sure it's wise. I don't want blood on my carpets. That was a joke," he added quickly.

"I thought it might be."

Polly was left in charge. She took her responsibility seriously and even managed to reprimand a huge bodybuilder, a former contender for the Strongest Man In The World title, who had forgotten to sign in. The reproof was accepted with dignity and the error remedied.

But most of her time was spent running errands. One of these was to the betting shop on behalf of Harry Hains, a small, slim man who showed astonishing agility on the parallel bars. He was a temporarily out of work circus trapeze artist who had told her that he was keeping in trim in anticipation of a call from the Russian State

Circus. The bet, a double, came up and he proved to be a generous tipper. Later, his thin and mole-like face triggered a chord in her memory and she was sure, or almost sure, that he had been in the group with Ronald Dent and Mr Heindrickson. She took a telephoned message for him to the effect that the long-awaited call from Russia still had not arrived and he sighed, but he tipped her another pound before leaving for the night.

It was a quiet evening. She had brought a meal of cold meat and salad from home. Most of the members left by mid-evening and by resorting to almost ferocious hinting Polly sent the last few stragglers on their way. On impulse, she borrowed the phone in Darryl's office. Her mother took the news that her daughter was alive and well with her customary calm. "Where are you calling from?" she asked.

"That's my business," said Polly. "And you needn't bother keying 1471, because I dialled 141 first, so you won't be given my number or anything else. I just thought I'd let you know that I've got a job and a place to stay and I'm not on the game, so you needn't worry about me – if that's what you were doing."

"Of course that's what I was doing." Mrs Turnbull's voice remained placid. "Darling, when are you coming home?"

"I'm not. Or not until you've got rid of Uncle Dick, or whoever it is next. It isn't home any more."

"Darling, I'm not ready yet to sit around and wait for death."

Polly could see her mother in her mind's eye, serene, forty and still beautiful, supremely confident that her magnetism for men would never let her go without. "Tell me when you are," Polly said. "Then maybe I'll come home and wheel you around in your bath-chair. I'll call you now and again." She broke the connection.

She went at the cleaning with renewed energy, working to exorcise the pain of hearing her mother's voice. Darryl had sown anxiety in her mind and the emptiness of the big space lent emphasis to her aloneness. In the night-time silence the old structure had its own noises which sounded like furtive footsteps and ghostly sniggering. The lens in the outer door showed little but blackness outside. She started the scooter inside the gym and managed, clumsily, to switch the lights off, open and close and lock the door without quitting the saddle. She shot out into the street like a dispatch rider and laughed at herself for needing the reassurance of lights and people.

Back at the house which she already thought of as 'home', the radio brought new life to the impersonal room. She carried it with her, listening at first to pop music and then light classics, as she went for a bath and then tidied her room in readiness for a visitor. She took the radio down to Darryl's room. He had offered her access to the washing machine and tumble drier in his kitchen alcove. She could have done her laundry at the gym but it seemed somehow indecorous to put her underwear in with the fighters' trunks and leotards, so she attended to her few items of laundry and put them away in the room.

With nothing left to occupy her, she braved the dark and fell fast asleep in Darryl's bed.

She was awoken by noises overhead. It took her several seconds to reorientate herself. It came to her that the noises were probably in her own room, but by the time she had climbed groggily out of Darryl's bed and found her slippers and the thin smock that served her as a dressing gown, the noises were out on the landing. She hurried into the hall. Something was descending the stairs. The muffled noises had resolved themselves into a continuous squawking of protest and the regular thumping made by a man being pulled downstairs by Darryl, who had a grip on one ankle.

The pair arrived in the hall with a final thump. Heads were appearing over the banisters. Casually, Darryl put his captive into a textbook leg-lock. "I caught a burglar, folks," he said. "The excitement's over. Go back to sleep."

Darryl was a forceful personality. He was also the landlord. Doors closed, reluctantly.

"Polly, meet Hugo Tyrone," Darryl said. "Not that that's his real name, but it'll do." He released the leg-lock and pulled the unfortunate Tyrone, still by one ankle, into his room, rolled him over again, knelt on his back and went through his pockets. Polly closed the door to keep the noise from disturbing the household again.

"Spare keys to the room upstairs and to the front door," Darryl said, tossing them onto the table. "And . . . get a load of this!" He put down, more carefully, a shining brass object. It seemed to be a curve of circles. "Brass knuckles," he said. He gave the unfortunate Tyrone a prod in the neck with a stiff forefinger that made the man yelp. "You're bloody lucky you didn't try them against me. I'd probably've killed you. I'd certainly have made you swallow them. And now, before I pull you like a wishbone – split you right up the middle – what've you got to say for yourself? Your tart robbed this young lady. So she took her money back and found she'd got a

51

bit extra. That's the luck of the draw and you'd no call to come round here with a set of knucks."

Darryl got to his feet. Tyrone, able to breathe again, took some seconds to find his voice. He was a slim man in his thirties with a lean and hungry face. His hair was oily and looked as though it was usually slicked down, but now it was erect in a cockscomb. "Christ's sake," he said painfully. "She can keep the money. It's peanuts. And I never reckoned revenge was worth the hassle." He began to roll over, as if to get to his feet.

"You stay down there," Darryl warned, "or I'll flatten you." Tyrone lay back against the carpet again. "Revenge?" he resumed. "You'd crawl over broken glass to pay back a grudge. Or to find a lost fiver. Why else would you have come here and put your balls on the line? Because that's what you did, know it or not. Whether you lose them this time around depends on you giving us the truth or not."

Tyrone's eyes were popping. "God's sake!" he snorted. "So Diana was out of line. She's like that. Greedy. But if somebody broke in here, beat up your girlfriend and took her money, wouldn't you do something about it?"

To Polly, the argument seemed perfectly reasonable. Darryl was in agreement, but for a different reason. He stooped over Tyrone and his expression was such that the intruder closed his eyes tightly. "I would," Darryl said. "I bloody well would. And that's what you came here to do, to beat her up and take her money. And, yes, I'm going to do something about it."

Darryl reached down with one hand. Tyrone, sensing the movement, opened his eyes and began a rapid crawl backwards over the carpet with his heels and elbows. "No, listen a moment," he said rapidly. "It wasn't for either of those things. I'm not short of cash and I've already made up the loss to Diana. But she went on and on at me – you know how a woman can nag? Diana's the world champ. It wasn't the money and it wasn't the poke in the gut, but she took a real fancy to that purse. It was quality goods, real class, she said. Nothing was going to satisfy her until she had it again. I reckoned I'd score some points if I got it back for her and maybe buy myself a little peace and quiet."

It was clear Darryl did not give much credence to this story and it seemed probable that he was about to implement one of his several threats. But Polly was seized by sudden inspiration. She had made up her mind not to be parted from her remaining cash. She could feel the purse in her dressing gown pocket, but she said, "Keep him there for a moment?"

"Sure," Darryl said. 'For ever, if needs be."

Polly picked up the extra keys and darted up the stairs. In her own room, she found a pencil and copied the number on the slip of paper in the purse onto a paper tissue. She returned downstairs. "You can't have the purse," she said. "It has sentimental value. But is this what you're really after?" She showed him the slip of paper.

She saw his involuntary movement before he shook his head. "Don't know what you're talking about," he croaked.

"Then it won't matter if I burn it?" Darryl's matches were on the table. She picked them up and opened the box, one-handed.

"Don't do that!" Tyrone said urgently.

"Then this is what you really want?"

"Give it to me anyway."

53

"Not until you answer me."

"Damn you! That's what I want. Give it to me."

"Why is it so important?"

"It's the combination to my mother's strongbox. She'll kill me if I lose it. And I'll make you suffer for this, one of these days," he added between clenched teeth.

Darryl had been listening in silence. Now he trod on Tyrone's foot, hard. Tyrone gasped and sat up. Darryl reached out and his big hands gripped Tyrone by the back of the neck and lifted him to his feet. The grip seemed to be paralysing. "I don't like that sort of talk," he said. He looked at Polly. "Shall we see how far up his arse we can push that paper with a billiard cue?"

"It's not worth going to war for a scrap of paper," Polly said. She tucked the slip of paper into a pocket of Tyrone's golf jacket. "Just get rid of him."

"Yeah. Listen." Darryl tightened his grip. Tyrone's eyes crossed and his tongue protruded. "If you come here or near either of us again," Darryl said, "I'll spike you on the nearest railings. Now, come to the top of the steps and we'll see how far I can throw you."

For the rest of the night, Polly slept in her own room. She shared Darryl's opinion that if Hugo Tyrone dared to return he would not know which room to invade. She rather thought that he would avoid that part of the city for years to come.

When they met in the morning, Polly asked curiously, "How far did you throw him?"

"I wasn't trying real hard. When I throw some crap-hound, I never put muscle into it unless I'm being paid. What was special about that piece of paper? The one in the purse?"

"There was a number on it."

"What sort of number?"

"I don't know. If it was a phone number it was a long one. Could have been a credit card number, I suppose, or a map reference. I copied it down."

Darryl's brow creased. "Why did you bother?"

"Again, I don't know. In case it ever matters. Beyond that, who cares?"

She spent the morning in the garden, pruning three rambler roses and forking over the empty spaces in the flowerbeds. There would be room to train some fruit trees on the garden walls and she had an idea to introduce a few more flowering shrubs and perhaps a Virginia creeper on the wall of the house. Darryl might be prepared to meet or at least share the cost if she spoke to him nicely.

The bathrooms were always empty around midday, which suited her very well. She took a shower and walked to the pub near the gym where she had a sandwich and a diet coke for lunch.

In the gym, after Darryl had worked out with another wrestler, gone through a series of strenuous exercises and had his own shower, they settled for a minute in the office. Polly had begun to help with the book-keeping, a chore which Darryl found both tedious and difficult. "You'll have to take charge for all of tomorrow," Darryl said. "I'm wrestling in Glasgow. It's a long ride and I'll want time for a rest at the end of it."

"Wouldn't you be better by train or plane?" Polly asked.

Darryl looked shocked. "Have you seem what they charge nowadays?" he demanded.

Polly had only the vaguest idea about fares so she

55

changed the subject. "Should you be wrestling so often?" she asked.

"Sometimes you sound exactly like my mother," Darryl grumbled.

Polly smiled for a moment at the prospect of having maternal feelings for a man who must be nearly ten years her senior. "But really," she said. "Don't they set a limit? Or are you allowed to fight every night until your health breaks down?"

He pulled a face expressive of great patience although she suspected that he was rather grateful that somebody cared. "We're graded by physique and popularity. I'm allowed to fight three times a fortnight. But they let you put in an extra bout if you're standing in for somebody who's sick or injured. We don't get brain damage like boxers. Kidney troubles, sometimes, from landing on your back so often, but that's rare."

"Okay," Polly said cheerfully. "In that case you can go. I'll look after the shop."

"Well, thank you, Mother."

She was about to tell him to ride carefully when the phone rang. Darryl picked it up, listened for a moment, grunted and broke the connection. "Tell Harry Hains that there's a message for him, about the Russian job. He can pick it up from his agent." Polly went out to where Hains was practising alone, on a trapeze that hung from the rafters for his sole benefit.

Polly awoke early in the morning to the sound of muted thunder as Darryl left on the big motorbike. By the light in the window it was nearly dawn. She rolled over, punched her pillow and went back to sleep, thinking of Darryl sweeping along the motorway.

A Running Jump

She spent another morning in the garden, forking old compost into the exposed areas of the beds. The cool of advancing autumn made the work more enjoyable. She started two new compost heaps, one of them for the leaves which had begun to fall from the beech trees overhanging the foot of the garden.

The new radio gave her companionship. It was tuned to a local station. This seemed to be offering a diet of low-grade pop. Polly's taste ran more to the popular classics or to good New Orleans jazz. She would have turned over if her hands had been clean. It was a relief when the music was interrupted and the news came on. Much of this was concerned with politics and she let her mind wander. Her attention was recaptured by news of a murder. Polly liked to think of herself as above such trivial and plebeian curiosity, but in fact, although the act of murder had been reduced in law to little more than a serious assault, Polly still experienced a *frisson* at the mention of the word. The discovery of the body was recent and the news coverage was sparse. An elderly man had been found dead in his top-floor flat. The only supplementary information so far available was that a visitor had arrived that morning and found the door ajar. This she had known to be unusual, so she had entered and found the body. She was said to be in a state of shock and being comforted by neighbours.

More details emerged later. The death scene was not far away and interest in so local a crime was such that the athletes in the gym that afternoon abandoned their exercises and gathered round Polly's radio when the local news came on. She was engulfed in the smell of male sweat, which she found simultaneously horrid and strangely exciting.

The dead man's name was released. He had been a Mister P (believed to be Patrick) Mahon. "Hey!" said Slasher. "I knew him, if it's the same. He was the beak at Southhill Comprehensive when I was there." He was hushed. The visitor and finder of his body had been a health visitor appointed to keep check on the wellbeing and continued survival of the elderly. Social Services had suffered criticism on several occasions when senior but deceased citizens had not been discovered until the attention of neighbours was drawn by the smell. On this occasion, they were faultless. The system had worked perfectly. But Mr Mahon was still dead.

It was confirmed that the dead man had been a retired headmaster. The police were not yet releasing any further details but the health visitor, a Mrs Justine Hicks, had left the scene after reporting the death by phone and had talked to a reporter while still in a state of shock and before the police had managed to catch up with her. The unfortunate Mr Mahon's body had been found on the floor of his sitting room. He had been securely bound and gagged but she had seen no obvious pointer to the cause of death. There were signs that the flat had been searched. The news finished and the music resumed. Polly turned it down.

"I was at Southhill Comprehensive too," said a black weightlifter, whose impressive physique drew many envious glances around the gym. "He was a good old boy."

"Fairly laid into you with the cane until the law changed," said Slasher. "He wouldn't get away with it nowadays."

"But he was fair," said the weightlifter. "Whatever he gave you, you'd asked for."

"That's true," Slasher said. "And if one of us got into trouble with the law, he'd fight like a tiger for us. Took some of us walking in the hills, now and again, I remember. He was a stickler for fresh air and exercise."

The weightlifter agreed. "Classroom windows open even in a black frost. Said it would toughen us up."

"Worked, didn't it?" said Slasher. He frowned. "Wasn't there talk of something valuable that'd come down through the family? An heirloom, like?"

The weightlifter nodded slowly. "So there was." His bass voice dropped even lower. "Maybe it was true, even. I wonder if they got away with it."

"If there ever was such a thing," said Slasher.

Four

According to all reports the police, for the moment, were remaining tight-lipped. The uttering of any official statement was delayed, no doubt until they thought that a little information might attract more in return. But somebody else was talking to the media. The six o'clock news added leaked information, thinly disguised as speculation, that the cause of death was smothering. Mr Mahon, apparently, had been silenced by a gag consisting of a golf ball, held in place by a cloth tied tightly round his face. This had covered his nose as well as his mouth. At first all would have been well, but as the cloth became soaked with saliva it had become impermeable to air and the unfortunate man's oxygen supply had been cut off. The legend of a valuable heirloom was now public knowledge and was referred to guardedly. It was suggested that the legend might have no basis in fact but that the intruders might have been misled into believing it. At the same time, there was mention of a report that an expert had visited Mr Mahon to give a valuation for insurance purposes and a rumour that his insurance premiums had been met from some unspecified but official source.

When the bulletin finished there was a silence that seemed unbreakable. "What a hell of a way to go," said a plump man who trained and managed two of the boxers. His sallow complexion was echoed by a suit which only just managed to be brown rather than yellow. There was a general murmur of agreement.

"But they're still calling it murder," said a bodybuilder who, so Polly had been told, worked as a stunt man and body double and also competed in Body Beautiful contests. "Sounds more like an accident. GBH, maybe, or manslaughter, but nobody meant to kill him. Can there be a murder charge if there was no intention to kill?"

"I don't think that matters," said a bantamweight boxer. "I think if somebody dies as a result of something criminal, I think the law treats it as murder. I think," he added doubtfully. The general opinion seemed to be that he was probably right, and if that wasn't the law it certainly should be.

Polly was surprised at the depth of feeling and the generally right-wing attitudes, but the company had been reinforced by several more former pupils of the late Mr Mahon and the manner of his death had sent a shockwave through their collective imagination. The attendance melted away rather earlier than usual and she was left to attend to her housekeeping duties. She had swept and tidied, washed out the showers and changing room and was dealing with the minor paperwork when there was a knock at the street door.

Polly jumped and bit her tongue. She was not generally a nervous type. The nature of her upbringing had taught her self-reliance where a more timid person might have started to jump at shadows. But being alone in a cavernous building on a dark night with an unidentified caller outside the door, after a night interrupted by the

vengeful Hugo Tyrone and an afternoon and evening
punctuated by news of a murder not far away, would
have daunted many a sturdier soul. Her terrors of that
fateful first evening returned in full measure. She had
already switched off most of the lights so that the
spreading area of the main hall was lit only by the
light from a street lamp, shining through a fanlight.

Polly approached the door and peeped through the
lens but in the darkness outside she could only distinguish
a pale blob of a face. "Who's there?" she called. She
was ashamed to discover that her voice came out as a
rabbit-like squeak. Her mother had been insistent that
one should never show fear. Predators, she said, could
smell it.

"It's me," said a voice. "Harry."

"Harry who?" Polly asked more firmly.

"Harry Hains."

It was only when Polly started breathing again that she
realised she had stopped. The conversation, she thought
in her relief, had the makings of a knock-knock joke, but
she could not think of a pun on Hains. She opened the
door on the chain until she could be sure that it was
indeed Hains and that he was alone. Only then did she
release the chain.

Hains appeared to be suffering from a similar nervous-
ness. His emaciated face looked bleached in the reflected
light of the street lamps. He seemed glad to close the door
behind him. "Glad I caught you," he said breathlessly. "I
just want to get something from my locker." He glanced
down at his small attaché case. "Sorry to be a nuisance.
Did I frighten you?"

"You did, a bit," Polly said. "All this talk about a
murder can get to you. Is it all right about the job?"

He jerked. "Job?"

"The circus," Polly said.

"Oh! No. The money wasn't good and I'd have been expected to double as a general labourer. They can keep their bloody job. I've other irons in the fire. There's always somebody has a fall or pulls a muscle and a replacement's needed in a hurry. Or else I can survive on the dole until the season starts again in the spring. Excuse me."

Polly went back to the office. She heard Hains at his locker. His footsteps returned to the outside door. She looked out to be sure that he pulled it to against the spring lock, then went back to making ticks in Darryl's register against the names of members who had used the facilities that day.

Darryl's system was simple and she finished up in a minute or two. She glanced around to make sure that all was ready for the next day and then headed for the door. This, although massive, had a wide gap underneath it, a fanlight above and a large keyhole to an old-fashioned lock, now disused.

Polly was wearing trainers and her footsteps were silent on the concrete floor. The two men outside were unaware of her approach. She heard a male voice speaking while she was still too far away to pick out the words but, as she neared the door, Harry Hains's voice came through clearly, whining and defensive. "It wasn't my fault," he said. "How was I to know that he'd be a dribbler?"

Polly could easily have eavesdropped on whatever was to follow, but she very much wanted not to hear any more. She backed silently away and sat down again in the darkened office. Her knees were shaking and breathing had become an effort. Surely, she thought, the words

couldn't mean what she thought they meant. She closed
her mind to the possibility and breathed deeply. She tried
to think pure and beautiful thoughts but no pure and
beautiful thought sprang to her mind at the moment.
She just wished that Darryl were here. Or her mother.
Or anybody.

When at last she had pulled herself together and
regained her nerve, she went to the door. There was
silence outside. The lens seemed to be showing empty
shadows. She listened intently for what seemed like
an hour and then opened the door, very quietly, just
a crack. Gathering courage, she opened it wider and
took a proper look.

The yard, and the street beyond, looked empty.

Back in the office there was just enough light for her to
consult Darryl's register of members. Then, snatching at
more deep breaths, she wheeled out the scooter, locked
up and set off home. As she rode, she tried to think
of an innocent explanation of Hains's words, but none
came to her.

She felt safe on the scooter which, she admitted to
herself, was probably illogical. Partly to postpone being
alone in her room or Darryl's flat she did a U-turn before
reaching home, bringing a taxi-driver one step closer to
his first coronary, and headed back through the middle
of the city. The headmaster's former pupils had kept up
a running discussion about the tragedy and, to settle
an argument, Slasher had produced a street map and
pointed to the block where Mr Mahon had lived. She
rode past. It was a busy street, brightly lit, and the face
of the building, a block of flats four storeys high, was
flat and featureless except for the pattern of windows.
Mr Mahon had lived on the topmost floor.

But the map had shown a back lane. Polly rode down an alley at the gable of the building. The back lane ran between the walled drying greens of the flats and the back of a church, deserted at that time of night. Polly could barely make out the detail of the flats apart from the few lighted windows. She rode the scooter through the lane, glad to have its lights to show a clear way and no horrors ahead, and came out in a side street and headed for home.

Wishing again that Darryl's physical and moral strength was at her side, she managed to walk the scooter up the steps. As she parked it in the hall, she heard the phone ringing in Darryl's flat.

He had left her a key to his flat, with permission to sleep in it if she was nervous about her own. She let herself in, wasting a second or two in making sure that both doors were locked behind her, and picked up the phone on the eleventh ring. Somebody was persistent.

The caller was Darryl himself. "I'm glad you answered," he said. "I've met a pal and I'm staying over. Another long ride tonight would be a bit too much. Just thought I'd let you know. I'll be back some time tomorrow. Everything all right?"

"More or less," she said. "Did you know there'd been a murder near here?"

"Happens all the time. Who was it?"

"A Mr Mahon. I think he was a head teacher somewhere."

"At Southhill Comprehensive," Darryl said quickly. "I was taught by him. He was a hard man but – by God! – he could teach. I'd be an ignorant bugger like the rest of them if it wasn't for him. And I liked the old sod. What happened to him?" Polly gave him the few facts that she had gleaned from the radio and heard him swear under his breath. "Shouldn't happen to a dog," he said at last. "I hope they get the bastards. But I must go. There's a taxi waiting." He hung up. Polly, who had been on the point of airing her doubts and indecisions, was left listening to the dialling tone. The receiver made a rattling sound as she replaced it.

The house was silent. Darryl's room had come to symbolise security to her and she decided to linger. To kill the silence, she switched on his television. The regional service was based in the city. A commercial break was finishing and an extended version of the News In Brief came on. The police had held a media conference at last and the details of the crime were confirmed, without adding much to what Polly already knew. A small but high-quality safe had been found standing open, confirming that the motive had been robbery but, because there had been no sign of a break-in, the police were working on the theory that at least one of the killers must have been known to the victim.

The shock came at the end. The heirloom was not only real, it had been well known to certain experts and because Mr Mahon had no close relatives it had been willed to the British Museum. Mr Mahon's great-grandfather had brought it back from China during the early 1860s. It comprised a vase of great rarity value. The television showed a photograph. Polly gasped. It was the same vase, even the same photograph, that the group around Ronald Dent had been studying so intently in the bar beneath the casino. The police were anxious to hear of its present whereabouts. A number for the incident room was given.

The weather forecast succeeded the news. Polly switched off the TV. All her fears and suppositions were amplified if not confirmed. But what to do? She needed advice. What would her mother have told her? But she could hear her mother's calm voice: '*Nobody can tell you what to do, my dear. You're a big girl now. Do whatever you think is right for you*'. Darryl, then. What would he say? But she already knew that. Minutes earlier, he had said, 'I hope they get the bastards'.

But the police were unlikely to 'get the bastards' while they were working on a false assumption. Her mind stumbled round and round the available facts, returning always to the central certainty. What she knew, the police would need to know.

Would the incident room be manned so late at night? Polly lifted Darryl's phone and put it down again quickly. Calls could be traced. There was a line between *helping the police* and *getting involved*, a line which she had no intention of crossing. Helping the police was a duty, getting involved was the high road to infinite inconvenience and expense, or worse – so ran the litany of her mother's friends. In this instance, getting involved might be dangerous.

There was a call box nearby. As a defensive bluff, Polly borrowed one of Darryl's coats and a broad-brimmed hat. She was almost the same height as the wrestler. The coat hung loosely around her but she hoped that her silhouette would be sufficiently masculine to deter predatory males such as her attackers of a few nights earlier. She made sure that she had coins before she left the house.

On an impulse, she walked past the first call box to another, several hundred yards further on. That, she thought, might complicate any attempt to identify her. There was a trace of early frost and her footsteps echoed in the empty street. The box was empty and the phone had been repaired since the last time it was vandalised.

The incident room phone number was busy. At Polly's fourth attempt, she was connected to a voice which identified itself as Detective Sergeant Something. The name was lost in what sounded like a yawn. "I have some information," Polly began.

"One moment," said the voice. "Can I have your name?"

"No," Polly said firmly. "You can't."

"Come now, Miss. Or is it Mrs?"

Suddenly Polly felt herself to be in command. "Nice try! It's Ms. Do you want my information or don't you?"

"Anything you can tell us. But it had better be checkable. Information loses half its credibility and nearly all of its value if we don't know the source. Give me a codename, so that we know who's talking if you call again."

Polly's mind went blank. She started to say 'Darryl', but checked herself. That would have been a bigger giveaway than her own name. She changed it to 'Daphne'.

"What do you have to tell us, Daphne?"

"If the late news had it right, you're working on the wrong lines. Mr Mahon needn't have known any of his attackers."

"If you know that much, you know that there was no sign of a break-in," the voice said patiently. "I can tell you a little more. The press will have it

69

by morning anyway. The victim was seen to return
home from the Social Club at around midnight. He
was known to be a cautious man. No way would
he have opened up for a stranger at that hour of
the night. His friends are unanimous about that. It
seems certain that he brought somebody back with
him."

"Are you telling me or am I telling you?" Polly
demanded severely. A man was passing in the street,
whistling slightly out of tune. She turned away and
hunched her shoulders. "Listen, would it change your
theory if I told you that there was a professional acrobat
involved?"

For the first time, the voice sounded fully awake. "Yes
it would. Who?"

"Harry Hains. He's a circus performer. He could have
climbed in while the flat was empty and opened the door
for one or more others. Mr Mahon was a fresh-air fiend
and usually left windows open."

"Hains's address?"

"I think he's staying at the YMCA. He was working
with Ronald Dent. You know Ronald Dent?"

"I think I can say that we do know Mr Dent." The
voice sounded amused.

"They definitely knew about the vase, they were
handling a photograph of it only a day or two earlier.
And they were in touch with an American antique dealer
named Heindrickson. I think that Mr Heindrickson is
or was staying at the Coronet Hotel. That's all I can
tell you."

Despite the late hour, the voice was becoming more
and more animated. "Listen, Miss – er – Ms. If this
checks out, you may have given us the break we need.

The chief will certainly want to talk with you. How can we get in touch again?"

"You can't," Polly said.

"But you may have a whole lot more to give us, more than you think you know. And there could be a reward—"

"I don't care." Polly saw a chance to drag a red herring across the path. "Use the reward to start a memorial fund. I just want to see my old headmaster avenged. He was a good man. He was tough but fair, and he couldn't half teach. But for him, I'd be an ignorant bugger like all the rest. Goodbye." She hung up and walked home, hoping that Darryl would have forgiven her for stealing his words. Nobody bothered her. She felt better. It was somebody else's problem now. She slept, in Darryl's bed, rather better than she had expected.

The morning seemed much like any other, or even more so. The sunshine had gone and the day was dull and damp with occasional spits of drizzle. The radio had nothing to add to the previous night's bulletin except that the police were following up a new lead. Even so oblique a reference made Polly feel exposed.

Back in her own room, she was interrupted at breakfast by the sound of the phone in the flat below. She raced downstairs, banishing from her mind any thought that either the police or Ronald Dent might have traced her. The phone was still shrilling when she reached it. The caller was Darryl. "You okay?" he asked.

"For the moment," Polly said.

Darryl ignored her reservation. "I've been asked to help coach a wrestling class at a youth club. If I do it,

I couldn't be back until late evening. Can you cope for another day? You won't lose by it."

"You don't have any compunction about leaving me to the mercy of all those fighters?"

She heard him laugh. "You're quite safe. Same reason that I don't get into fights. The law goes very hard on a wrestler who molests women."

Polly wanted to tell him to rush home, that she needed help and advice and possibly protection. But a moment's thought assured her that she was in no danger yet and that the only unwise course of action would be to depart from whatever was becoming the norm. She assured Darryl that she could manage perfectly well.

"Any news about Mr Mahon's killer?" he asked. She said that she might have a lot to tell him when he returned. Perhaps, she thought, that might hurry him up a little.

The dedicated gardener is not put off by a little rain. As she worked in the garden, lifting and dividing some rock-plants and an old clump of delphiniums, the radio (secure and dry in a polythene bag) kept her in touch with such news as the police were releasing. In the late morning, it was announced that two men had been questioned in connection with Mr Mahon's death and one of them had been detained. Later, there was an urgent appeal for the informant known as Daphne to phone the incident room again. Polly gritted her teeth. The police, not always known for their eagerness to disgorge information, were being regrettably forthcoming. Perhaps if she had admitted her identity there would have been less publicity. On the other hand, her mother would certainly have discovered her whereabouts and word might still have leaked out of the incident room to even more threatening beings. Such things, she had heard, had been known.

During the afternoon, the name of the man in custody was released. By this time, Polly's radio was in the middle of the big gymnasium and with the volume turned up to maximum. At every mention of the murder, activity was suspended. Ronald Dent's name was mentioned but occasioned no more than a few knowing nods, but when Harry Hains was named there was a general murmur of interest. He was known to most of the company. "Who'd've thought the little bugger had it in him," Slasher said when the music resumed. Polly turned the volume down.

"I dunno," one of the boxers said indistinctly. With his gumshield out, his lack of teeth made itself obvious. "He was always on the lookout for a chance to make an easy quid or two."

"He was generous with it," Polly said.

"Easy come, easy go," said the boxer. "And it fits together, sort of. I've been to old Mahon's flat – when I was a prefect, that was – and he had more locks and bolts on the door than Wormwood Scrubs, but his windows were just the way they were built. Anyone who could reach the windowsills three floors up could have opened them with a lollipop stick. That's if they were shut at all. I never saw what looked like an heirloom brought back from China, but that doesn't mean it wasn't there. I reckon they'd need a good spiderman to climb up and let the others in. Then they could be waiting for him when he got home."

His sparring partner grunted agreement. "I never believed that tale about the Russian circus. They got enough artists of their own and Harry's nothing out of the ordinary. I reckon it was just a way of passing messages to let him know if the job was on that night or not. Who were the messages from?" he asked Polly.

For a moment Polly thought that her involvement was common knowledge. Then she steadied. "No idea," she said. "Just a voice on the phone. They never said who was calling. At first they were saying that there was nothing for him. Then, the day before yesterday, there'd been a message from Russia and he could pick it up from his agent."

"There you are, then. A code to tell him the job was on that night."

The conversation died and other noises resumed, the regular beat of skipping, thumps from the punch-bags, grunts as the machines were put to use and a whole cacophony of gasps and thuds as two wrestlers worked out on the mat. Then a gymnast broke a bone in his hand and needed treatment at Casualty. Nobody else had transport available, so Polly took him on the pillion of the scooter. He was free with his good hand and she told him he could walk home or take the bus.

"You're not going to wait for me, then?"

"Not unless they've found a cure for wandering hands."

When she got back to the gymnasium there had been a call from Darryl. He had not left a message. Polly prayed that the call had not been to say that he was staying away for another night. In mid-evening Darryl phoned again. "I'm on my way," he said. "Any news about Mr Mahon?"

"Some," Polly said.

"I could use a pint. Meet me at home at eleven and we'll have a beer and a chat."

The big motorcycle was already standing in the hall, emitting smells of hot metal and engine oil, when Polly rode the scooter up the shallow steps and inside. The front door had been left ajar for her. Darryl had removed his leathers and was neat and clean in a polo neck, tweed jacket and green corduroy trousers. The clothes had been bought off the peg to accommodate the girth of his sturdy build, so that the legs and sleeves were just long enough to look slightly comical and he had cultivated the habit of hitching up the trousers almost painfully tightly and keeping his elbows slightly bent. Polly decided that one day she would take most of Darryl's clothes for alteration or even, at a pinch, tackle the job herself.

"Come on," Darryl said. "We'll go to the casino." Polly had reservations about returning to where she had first encountered Ronald Dent and his companions, but Darryl misunderstood her hesitation. "It's all right," he said. "It's my round again. I owe you for looking after the gym."

Her breath was taken away by the assumption that a half-pint of shandy would be adequate recompense for almost two days sole responsibility, but she managed to protest that she was not dressed for the casino. Darryl was in no mood to wait while she changed. "They don't mind if you're in dungarees or a diving suit as long as you don't go up to the gaming rooms," he said. "Up there, it's party frock or collar-and-tie or you don't get in." Polly forgot to make any other objection as he swept her out of the house and down and across the street.

The bar below the casino was less empty than on

the previous occasion. Several couples were apparently exchanging telepathic messages of lust and a winner was celebrating with a trio of friends. The women were dressed to the nines so that Polly felt like Cinderella among far from ugly sisters.

Darryl fetched a beer and a shandy from the bar and they settled down. To break the ice, Polly asked how he had got on. "Piece of cake," he said. "How's everything been here?"

Polly was ready to pour out all her fears and suspicions, but at that moment they were joined by a statuesque lady, a genuine but tinted blonde in black velvet, who Darryl introduced as Mrs Franklyn, wife of the manager. Polly felt an instant warmth for the woman, who managed to combine a dignified bearing with an air of jollity, so she contained herself in patience and made conversation until Mrs Franklyn moved on to greet the drinkers and gamblers at another table.

"Now, for God's sake listen," she said. Some good piano jazz was being dispensed at moderate volume over the speakers so they were in no danger of being overheard, but Polly lowered her voice as she described the stages by which she had become sure of the identities of Patrick Mahon's assailants.

"So what are you going to do?" Darryl asked her.

"I've already done it. I phoned the police."

"You did *what*?" Darryl managed not to raise his voice.

"I had to," Polly said, almost pleadingly. "They were assuming that at least one of the robbers was known to Mr Mahon and that he'd brought him, or them, home with him. If that was a false assumption, they'd never

76

have arrested anybody. And you said you hoped they'd get the bastards."

"I didn't say to get your head in a sling."

"Well, my head isn't in a sling yet and I don't think it will be. I didn't tell them my name. I phoned from a call box, not even the nearest one."

"They must know that you could have seen the picture. And you carried the messages to Harry Hains. Ronald Dent's dangerous company and he doesn't forgive in a hurry."

"It said on the radio that he'd been arrested."

"Not arrested. Questioned. Not the same thing at all. Don't look round and whatever you do don't look scared. He's just walked in."

Polly managed not to look round. "How could he get out so soon?" she asked indignantly.

"Very easily."

"But I told the police about him looking at the picture of Mr Mahon's vase with Harry Hains and Mr Heindrickson and another man."

"That wouldn't necessarily make him guilty. The law requires more positive proof than that. The police would have to release him or charge him and they don't have half enough to charge him with, not on the unsupported evidence of an anonymous informant. He wouldn't have gone on the robbery, that isn't his style at all. Nowadays, he prefers to get other suckers to do the dirty work and take the risks. The police will leave him alone while they try to get the evidence they need. Or find witnesses. And that means you."

"I don't think I like what I'm hearing," Polly said.

"I don't want to panic you," Darryl said, smiling with determination, "but think about this. If the police start wondering whether the three you named were seen together and if they come here and if – another if – Ronnie Dent gets to hear of it, it may help him to remember that we were in here that night."

"Can we get out of here, please?" Polly asked in a small voice.

"Finish your drink, slowly. And smile."

Five

That night Polly was restless. In her dreams saw the harsh features of Ronald Dent and twice she awoke with a start.

She had tried to look unruffled and avoid any expression of triumph or fear while they unhurriedly finished their drinks and strolled outside. The man had been in a visibly stormy mood and on the one occasion when she dared glance round Polly thought he seemed to be looking in her direction. Darryl told her she was letting her imagination run away with her. As they left, she was sure that she could feel his eyes on her back, like the glow from a hot bulb.

Darryl waited until they were inside the house. He drew her into his room and put on the kettle before breaking his silence. "Okay," he said at last. "You didn't tell the police who you were. Probably just as well – these things leak out. But by *not* telling them who you were you may have attracted more attention, made it more difficult for the fuzz to make a case – because they don't know about you overhearing what Harry Hains said – and that way making sure that at least one bad bugger's still walking around free. And we don't know who else was in it."

"I had worked all that out for myself," Polly said

humbly. "And they couldn't have used what I overheard anyway. That would have been hearsay evidence."

"Well, work this out." He threw himself backwards into an armchair so that the joints protested, but his posture was far from relaxed. Polly wondered whose safety he was nervous for. "We've no way of knowing whether Ronnie Dent's rumbled you or not. He may never figure out who the snitch is but he may have put it together already. Maybe you'd better go back where you came from."

Polly thought that over. For a moment, the memory of her old bedroom and her mother's loving if casual care brought a flood of nostalgia. But then she shook her head. She had no intention of crawling home with her tail between her legs, to be exposed to the attentions of her mother's current lover. She felt revulsion at the thought of becoming a child again. Conversely, she had come to enjoy the comparative independence of her new life and the sense of adventure that it brought her. And she was developing an inexplicable fondness for Darryl and all his clientele. The kettle came to the boil and Darryl got up to make a pot of tea.

"I can't go back," she said.

"Why not? Have you done something awful?"

She snorted inelegantly. "Any day now, if you go on trying to get rid of me. But I just can't."

Darryl's brow creased. "I'm not trying to get rid of you, but I want you safe and I want you to *feel* safe. I can't relax with a jittery female about the place. So how about moving on to somewhere new?" He paused and swallowed. "I could give you some money to get you started." The words seemed to have been dragged out of him.

Polly jumped to her feet and kissed him on the cheek. They sat down again. Darryl inspected the brew. He looked rather pink. "Thanks," Polly said. "But no thanks. I might not be so lucky next time. I do feel safe here with you to look after me and I can always disclose myself to the cops and ask for protection if we think that I'm in any danger. Somewhere else, I might not meet up with somebody I could trust."

"Well, all right," Darryl said slowly. "But you'd better stick close to me. Real close. Dent doesn't go in for firearms and I can deal with most other sorts of violence. It's what I'm good at. Come into my bed if you like. I wouldn't touch you."

Polly basked for a moment in the warmth of the offer. "I know you wouldn't, bless you," she said. "But it isn't necessary. I feel quite safe, knowing that you're downstairs."

Darryl sat up a little straighter. "And I don't want you alone in the garden all morning."

"You could always give me a hand in the garden," Polly pointed out. "With me to help you, you don't need to spend so long at the gym. There's a dump of old stones behind the greenhouse and I want to extend and rebuild a small retaining wall and a rockery and change the levels a bit."

"I could do that, I suppose. But flowers take one look at me and shrivel up."

"I feel the same. I'll do the planting," Polly promised. "But I could use a strong back to help with the heavy stuff. And now, I'd kill for a cup of that tea."

The police were making no more public statements, but somehow a lot was known. Tiny scraps of knowledge were passed around and brought together and pondered over in the public consciousness and out of it all emerged rumour often founded securely on fact. The word was that Harry Hains had grazed his wrist climbing in at the window of Patrick Mahon's flat and left a trace of blood which, once they knew where to look, the police had managed to detect even on the red brick of the wall and which the Forensic Science Laboratory, moving at unusual speed, had matched to his DNA. The CPS had therefore felt able to charge him with complicity and he remained in custody, saying nothing to any good purpose. There was no hard evidence to implicate Ronald Dent, but everybody knew of his guilt. The police were appealing for witnesses who had been in the vicinity of Mr Mahon's flat at the crucial time. They were asking a great many questions and living in hope although it was more than possible that the other assailants had been one or more of Dent's minions and had not included Dent himself.

Dent also was asking a great many questions, but nobody seemed to know the identity of the mysterious Daphne.

For a week, Polly and Darryl lived in each other's pockets. Darryl never left her without making sure that she would be in the company of others and knew how to contact him in an emergency. Most days, they lunched in the carvery at the Coronet Hotel. But when Darryl proposed a late-night visit to the bar at the casino, Polly jibbed. "Ronald Dent might be there," she pointed out.

"All the more reason. If he sees that you're avoiding him, it may start him thinking." Polly had rather hoped that out of sight might be out of mind but she allowed

herself to be persuaded. To her relief, there was no
sign of Dent in the big basement bar. The room was
almost empty, although from the state of the ashtrays it
seemed that it had been busy earlier. The manager and
part-proprietor was sampling a liqueur at the bar but
came over to join them. Darryl introduced him to Polly.
Mr Franklyn was of less than average height but made
up for it in girth. Despite being definitely pear-shaped
he was well dressed and turned out. He was largely bald
but had refrained from drawing strands of his remaining
hair across the gap. His round face was highly coloured
and etched with smiling lines. Polly decided that she
liked him. "I met your wife in here the other evening,"
Polly said. "She's very attractive."

"Isn't she just!" Mr Franklyn looked surprised and
pleased. He beamed and pulled up a chair. "Silver
wedding next month, but you'd never know it, would
you?"

"Not in a million years," Polly said obligingly.

"She could still get into her wedding dress. And you
wouldn't believe what a help she is in the business. A
woman's viewpoint . . . We'd like to have more lady
visitors and more young men. The men don't seem to
take their wives gambling around here. At the moment
the players are mostly male and over-forties – except for
blokes showing off to a new girlfriend, and the Chinese,
of course. They're great gamblers, the Chinese, all of
them." He sighed. "If only they'd interbreed with the
Brits." Mr Franklyn was silent for a moment, lost in
a dream of a perfect world. "But they keep themselves
to themselves. Now, I must be getting on. Have the
next round on the house." He had a brief word with
the dignified lady behind the bar on his way out.

"Now, I call that clever," Darryl said. "He eats out of his wife's hand, and maybe any other places he can get to." He seemed to feel that Polly had discovered, in admiring Mrs Franklyn, the Open Sesame to free drinks. He went to the bar and returned with the fresh supplies. "I'm wrestling on Saturday," he said. "Be away all afternoon and well into the night. I thought I might get Slasher to babysit you. I know there hasn't been any sign from Dent, but you wouldn't expect him to send up smoke-signals, now would you?"

"I suppose not." As the days passed, Polly had begun to forget about any possible danger from Ronald Dent, relishing instead all the new experiences and sensations that were coming to her, but Darryl's question whipped away her fragile sense of security. She set aside her resentment at the reference to babysitting. "Couldn't I come with you?" she asked.

"You're sure you could stand it for three hours each way on the pillion?"

"I can if you can."

"Sure?"

"Positive."

Darryl considered. "I don't see why not," he said at last. "Slasher can look after the shop for a day and we'll have time on Sunday to sort out any muddles he's got himself into. Wear all the clothes you've got. It'll be cold."

Polly had proved popular with the clients at the gym, who for the most part were open-handed. Despite Darryl's thriftiness, Polly's little nest-egg had continued to grow, thanks largely to the tips that she earned. In addition to running errands and taking messages, for example, she had undertaken that any sweaty trunks or leotards left on the windowsills would be washed and tumble-dried ready for the next day. She also kept a stock of soft drinks, obtained from the cash-and-carry, for re-sale to anyone who had sweated himself into a state of thirst. These little services were appreciated.

As a result of all these endeavours, she could afford to shop again, in a modest way, for clothes. She had had it in mind to stock up with warmer outfits in preparation for winter. She had no intention of buying motorcycle gear which might never be worn again, but nor did she intend to risk expensive but delicate clothes on Darryl's pillion. She was fortunate in finding, in her favourite thrift shop and at a bargain price, a knee-length coat of russet leather which fitted her very well. She would have liked trousers to match, but that was too much to hope for. Instead, along with a small but carefully chosen selection of winter clothes, she acquired a pair of waxproofed trousers and a pair of suede ankle-boots.

Thus kitted out and wearing Darryl's spare helmet, when they set off on the Saturday morning she was perfectly warm and even the rain which followed them for fifty miles did little to spoil her comfort. Motorway speeds, which at first had turned the world into a passing blur, soon began to seem quite slow.

They pulled off the motorway near the halfway point, for a rest and refreshment. Polly ate a sticky bun but Darryl took only tea. "If I'm going to get hit in the stomach," he said, "I'd prefer it empty. We'll go for a carry-out before we start back."

Polly had become aware of a growing concern for Darryl. She had witnessed several genuine injuries being inflicted in the ring. "How much of a risk are you taking?" she asked. "Sometimes, as a spectator, it's seemed to be a true contest. Other times, it all looks faked. Which is nearer the truth?"

He shrugged. "Sometimes," he said, "you get two old pals throwing each other around to please the crowd. And often, by agreement, two wrestlers will go through routines that let each of them show off his strongest moves. Remember, Polly, a genuine contest may mean a lot to the contestants but it may not look good to the crowd – unless there appears to be some real needle between them, which happens very easily. Then again, you may come to an agreement to spend the first, say, three rounds doing the showy moves and after that may the best man win. It's different every time and there's no hard and fast rules about it."

"And this time?" she asked.

He looked suddenly less cheerful. "This one's going to be a bastard," he said. "It's the main bout and good money or I wouldn't have taken it on. It's going to be on satellite television."

"That means valuable exposure?"

"That means an extra fee. But I'm up against Frankie Delrose."

Polly gave vent to a low whistle. "I've seen him," she said. "He doesn't often lose."

"He hates above anything to lose on telly. And you can't trust him. We'll probably start off with some agreement for the opening rounds, but I'll be watching out from the first bell. I won't even shake hands with him at all – he's been known to pull his opponent onto a forearm smash. He's a hard man to beat."

"But you can do it," Polly said, more to reassure herself than him.

"Sometimes Frankie loses his temper," Darryl said. "That makes him dangerous but also it makes him careless. It can pay to get him wild, provided you're ready for all hell to break loose."

"If he was giving you a really hard time, would you let him have an easy win?"

Darryl looked shocked. "You're joking! The public will be coming in the hope of seeing me beat him, or at least of seeing blood and snot all over the ring. It's what they cough up good money for and that's what pays my fees. If I lose my reputation for putting up a damn good fight my fees will go down, I'll get fewer fights and I'll end up on the scrapheap. If I see that I'm going to lose the bout, I'll try to lose it in a way that makes me look good and him look bad."

"You can't do that, can you?"

"There's ways and ways, if you're prepared to bend the rules a little," said Darryl. He paused. "Dirty tricks reminds me. Did we disturb you last night?"

"I was sort of restless but I don't remember hearing anything. Why? What happened?"

"Ronnie Dent came knocking at the door."

The mention of the name was enough to bring Polly's anxiety flooding back. "I dreamed about him. At least, I thought it was a dream but it may have been telepathy or something. What did he want?"

"Telepathy be damned. You probably heard his voice at too low a level to recognise. Subliminal, they call it. He still wants me to deliver something. Only money, he said. It'd be the thin end of the wedge. I told him to go bowl his hoop."

87

"You're sure that he wasn't really suspicious? Of me?"

"It had nothing to do with you." Darryl gave her a reassuring pat on the hand. "I've been thinking about it. Unless you're careless, there's only one way he could get a lead to you and that's through the cops. And that won't happen if you watch what you say to them."

"I shan't say anything to them ever again," Polly said fervently.

"You will, you know. They'll be investigating everything Harry Hains did during the days before the killing. Twenty people at least must know that you were taking telephone messages for him. They're bound to want to talk to you. When they get around to it, just make sure you don't let slip anything they wouldn't expect you to know. If they find out who Daphne is, it's bound to get out." He stood up and began to fasten his leathers. "Come on. I want time for a rest, a hot shower and a loosen up before the bout."

Polly had been enjoying the smooth speed of the ride but her pleasure was spoiled. For the remainder of the journey her mind picked at the bad luck and her own rashness that had stolen her security and peace of mind.

Their destination was a town hall, built between the wars but with classical pretensions. For security, Darryl was allowed to take the motorbike into the rear foyer, lined and floored with imitation marble. He gave Polly a ticket which, he said, would put her beside his corner, and disappeared up some stairs. She locked her surplus clothing in one of the panniers. Then she was free and she had time in hand. She went out to post a card to her mother and had a snack in a nearby café.

*   *   *

A Running Jump

The big hall was almost full when she took her seat. Moments later, an official was stooping to speak to her. "Darryl Davidson wants to speak to you. Come this way." The official sounded disapproving, as though he resented being used as a go-between in a wrestler's amours. He led her to a door at the head of an aisle. "This is as far as you go," he said. "It leads to the dressing rooms."

Darryl, wrapped in a glossy blue dressing gown, was waiting behind the door, at the foot of a staircase. His manner was nervous. "Listen," he said. "The usual second has gone down with flu. I'm not having the bugger they've substituted. He's a pal of Delrose."

"So—?" Polly had a sudden sense of impending doom.

"So, you'll have to do it. Don't look so dumbstruck, there's nothing to it. You just hand me the towel and the water bottle."

"That's really all?"

"That's the lot. I never let anyone else come close – I've had a second poke a finger my eye before now."

"On purpose?"

"I still haven't been able to work that one out. You can talk to me between rounds. In theory, you're supposed to escort me back to the dressing room and stay between me and my opponent in case the fight breaks out again, but we'll let you off that chore. Up there will be full of naked wrestlers. Can you manage?"

The first principle in Polly's life was never to admit that there was anything she couldn't do. "I suppose so," she said. She hurried back to her seat as the lights went up over the ring and the MC started to fiddle with the microphone.

The opening bouts seemed to please the crowd. She was aware, as if from a distance, of the sounds of battle and of applause and occasional booing. She had a touch of anticipatory stagefright, but that was a minor distraction. Another concern was that the event was being recorded for television and surely the main bout would be the one most likely to be broadcast. As she returned to her seat she had seen at least three cameras at balcony level but there seemed to be no cameras staring into her face. Perhaps if she kept facing her front . . . And it was unlikely that her mother would be watching. Once a devotee, she had lost all fondness for wrestling as a spectator sport when that particular 'uncle' had let her down. Below and above these thoughts was a mounting anger at fate. To add to her other woes, she was now pitchforked into acting as Darryl's second, a role that she might have enjoyed at any other time . . . if she had had warning to dress for it instead of looking like a protester on an ecological sit-in.

The earlier bouts slipped away and were gone. The MC announced the main bout. The crowd stirred. This was what they had come to enjoy. Darryl's name was greeted with applause, his opponent's with boos and catcalls. The two wrestlers entered. As Darryl had said, they both looked larger, up in the ring. Frankie Delrose, she thought, had a slight advantage in weight and he seemed to be built of solid slabs of muscle, but he was older than Darryl and looked less agile.

To the evident surprise of her neighbours, Polly got out of her seat. She thought she must be blushing scarlet but she climbed the few steps, took Darryl's gown from him and leaned over the top rope to offer a few words of encouragement. Stripped to his trunks, Darryl revealed a great deal of muscle – not the snake-like muscles of the bodybuilder but the smooth plates denoting real strength. He asked for the water bottle and rinsed his dry mouth while the referee, a retired lightweight wrestler, climbed into the ring and repeated the introductions. Polly backed to her seat, an object of curiosity. The referee uttered a few words of caution and stepped back. The bell sounded.

The first round produced no fireworks. The wrestlers went through well-grooved routines, settling in and feeling each other's strength. Polly thought each would be waiting for the other to show signs of tiredness.

The bell sounded again. Darryl returned to his corner. He had worked hard but he was breathing easily. Polly handed him the towel and the water bottle and told him that he was looking good. He seemed hardly aware of her presence but to be focused entirely on the bout.

Midway through the second round, there was a sudden flurry. Darryl took an unexpected blow to the stomach and went down. To Polly the blow had looked like a legitimate forearm and with no great force behind it. The referee started counting. Darryl got to his knees and mimed a punch. The referee and most of the crowd had been unsighted. The crowed booed and the referee gave an informal warning to Delrose, who had replied, indignantly miming a forearm smash. The referee signalled for the bout to continue.

The incident should have passed off. Delrose had lost nothing but face. He had not been penalised. He could not lose the sympathy of the crowd because it had never been with him. Nevertheless, he was clearly furious and

Polly realised that this had been a deliberate tactic on Darryl's part. Darryl was still straightening up when Delrose rushed at him. But Darryl was waiting for the rush, ready with a throw that sent the other man skidding against a corner post. What was left of Delrose's temper went to the winds and he flew at Darryl, again and again, in uncontrolled charges which were meant to sweep his opponent off his feet or batter him against a corner post, but in fact left himself open to equally violent counter-moves, the last of which was a hip-throw into a pinfall position. He struggled, but Darryl held him for the count of three.

While Darryl mopped himself and wetted his mouth again, Frankie Delrose remained on his feet. His chest was heaving and he glared at Darryl. "Be careful," Polly said. "He's good and mad but he's started thinking again."

Darryl nodded. "And he can't afford to lose another point."

The bell sounded for the third round. Delrose approached Darryl with a friendly smile and his hand extended for a shake, but Darryl circled out of reach. Delrose pretended to turn away in disgust but span back and launched a sudden attack for which Darryl was only half ready. Darryl met a body-check which put him down for a moment. He took his time to recover his breath and got up on the count of nine only to meet another charge and body-check. Again Darryl was bowled over, but this time landed on his back. His right leg was up on the middle rope.

Delrose threw himself down with all his weight behind his knee on Darryl's leg. Darryl's cry of pain was drowned in a roar from the crowd. The referee pulled at Delrose but the wrestler back-handed the referee and rolled his weight to and fro on Darryl's leg.

The crowd was becoming frantic but nobody was doing anything. The referee was dazed and the other second, who should have been rushing to restrain his principal, was hesitating. Polly could not hear Darryl's voice but she was in no doubt that he was injured and that whatever his injury might be it was being aggravated. Moreover, he was clearly in agony. Her anger boiled over. Before she had time to think she found that she had bolted from her seat, shot up the steps and vaulted over the top rope. She rushed at Delrose, furious, uncertain what to do but knowing that somebody had to do something. The voice of the crowd rose to a crescendo. At the last moment, instinct took over where reason had run out of time. She arrived at speed, swinging her leg in an explosion of fury. Her knee caught the wrestler just below his ear and bowled him over, half stunned. The crowd erupted in cheers and clapping.

Polly was hurt. She had not expected a head to offer so much resistance and she feared for a moment that the first-aiders might have more than one broken leg to deal with. But she ignored the pain and knelt on her other knee beside Darryl.

Darryl was grey with pain but had his wits about him. "Slowly," he said. "Straighten my leg and lift it down. Take its weight all the way." She did so. "Better," he said. "Lay it down gently." He gripped her hand until she could envisage more broken bones.

"Should I have done what I did?" she asked him. "Or was I too impetuous again?" Her anger had found its outlet and gone. She had forgotten altogether about keeping her face away from the cameras.

Darryl's voice had sunk to a whisper as the pain took hold. "You couldn't have done better. You're a marvel. Who's supposed to be looking after who?"

Delrose and the referee were on their feet again and this time Delrose was being restrained by his second and the referee. Polly thought that he was putting on an act for the crowd. He could easily have shaken off the two men if he had been so minded, but to attack a woman in the ring would have invited the most hostile publicity and Polly was beginning to sense that Delrose's public face was calculated to do no more than earn him the highest possible fees. He allowed himself to be led away. His second was hard put to it to prevent assault by several members of the audience but Delrose ran for the door to the dressing rooms. When the noise died down the referee announced his disqualification.

The national anthem was being played through the speaker system but people were already making for the doors. Darryl was lifted carefully onto a stretcher. A small core of enthusiasts remained and Polly found her hand being shaken and her back slapped. She even signed several autographs. There were questions which she ignored. She followed the stretcher.

Darryl was carried into the rear foyer and splints were applied. An ambulance had been summoned. Somebody brought down his clothes from the changing room. The first few wrestlers to leave came down the stairs and paused to promise that there would be a whip-round. "They always say that," Darryl told her. His voice was sleepy, Polly guessed from the effect of painkillers. "Sometimes it really happens. Listen." He fumbled in the bundle of clothes. "Here's the key for the bike. You'll have to ride it back for me."

Polly was horrified. "Darryl, I *can't*."

Darryl's voice was recovering strength. "Well, I sure as hell can't. And if it sits here there won't be much of it, if anything, left by the time I can ride again. You can ride the scooter so you can manage the bike."

"Couldn't I take it back on the train?"

Darryl frowned. "I've been here by train. You'd have to change trains at least once, probably twice. That's if you could make the connections at this time of night. Do you reckon you could heave it in and out of guards' vans?"

"I could get a porter—"

"At this time of night? Or any other time, come to that. Porters have gone the way of the dodo. If you're worried about being home alone, go to a hotel somewhere. I'll pay." The ambulance had arrived. Two men prepared to lift Darryl. They looked too frail for his sturdy frame but they raised him with the ease of long practice. "You've done brilliantly so far. Don't let me down now." As they lifted him into the ambulance, Darryl was still giving her instructions about the positive stop gear-change.

The doors closed and the ambulance moved away.

Six

Polly's head was swimming. She had absorbed everything the day had managed to throw at her so far, but being expected to ride a powerful motorcycle a matter of nearly two hundred miles in the dark would have been definitely over the top, even if she had ignored the facts that she had no insurance, no valid driving licence and had enough trouble mastering the scooter over short distances. She found that she was still holding Darryl's robe. She folded it carefully and put it away in one of the panniers.

She was still hesitating in the foyer when Frankie Delrose came down the stairs, very dapper in a suede car coat and a neat homburg. There was a large flower in his buttonhole. The side of his face was swollen and beginning to discolour, but she had found that fighters soon learned to ignore such injuries or even, up to a point, pain itself. Delrose seemed to be well pleased with his evening. He stopped in front of Polly and put out his hand. Polly put her hands behind her back. Delrose laughed a laugh like the braying of a donkey. He took her face in his hands and kissed her lingeringly on the lips. In her confusion, she was visited by the mad thought that this was a mere trick to get her to bring her hands out from behind her back, so she kept them there. She was surprised to find that he was no taller than she was. Delrose finished the kiss and pulled away. "No hard feelings?" he said.

Polly found her voice. "Not on my part. I can't speak for Darryl. You're the one I expected to have hard feelings."

He laughed again, a dirty laugh. "Not the way you mean. It'll be great publicity. They'll come in droves, hoping to see it happen again. For a hundred quid, come and repeat it at Salford next week."

"I'd like to," Polly said. She found that she was feeling quite at ease with him and she could have used the money. 'I'd like to do it again and much, much harder. But it hurts my knee too much."

His braying laugh echoed around the marbled hall. "Then come and be my second." Polly said that she was already committed to Darryl. "Not tonight, you're not. Come and have dinner with me. You're a girl with guts. I like that. And you owe me."

Polly's appetite had returned with a vengeance. She was almost tempted to accept the meal until she remembered that this was the man who had injured Darryl. The monster in the ring had seemed quite separate from the humorous little vulgarian who was chatting her up. "I don't owe you a damn thing," she said. "Except maybe another kick in the head."

"That's the trouble with being the baddy," he said, feigning sadness. "You don't get your share of the girls. So long!" He walked out into the street.

That settled it for Polly. If she could floor a notorious wrestler to public acclaim and then be kissed by him, she could ride anything, even a powerful and expensive motorbike. This time, she would not have Darryl in front of her to part the wind. She wrapped herself up again and donned Darryl's leathers over the top. They were long enough but loose. She felt as fat as the Michelin man but at least she should be warm. She was sweating already.

She was struggling with the weight of the bike when the last pair of wrestlers descended. They were in high spirits, partly accounted for by the beery smell that followed them down the stairs, and they were full of admiration. One of them hugged Polly while the other raised her hand in triumph. Hers had been the performance of the evening, they said. They had seen it on a miniature television in the changing room. They invited her to come and act as their seconds at any time. They wheeled the machine into the street for her, pointed out her easiest route to the motorway, supported the weight for her while she mounted, showed her how to start the engine and waved until she was out of sight.

The motorbike handled like an upscaled version of the scooter. It was an advantage that she had travelled on the pillion and had a feel for the balance of it. Once she was moving it seemed to balance itself but eventually she would have to come to a halt and she was far from confident that she could support its weight. Fortunately, her route to the motorway was short and passed only two sets of traffic lights. The first of these was in her favour. At the second, there was no traffic approaching so she simply went through on the red. The few pedestrians paid no attention. Such behaviour was only to be expected.

Polly already knew to be gentle with the throttle. When she had progressed up the gears, she found the machine almost docile. She joined the motorway and picked up cruising speed. The loose leathers whirred maddeningly in the wind but she shut the distraction out of her mind. Soon, she even found the confidence to change lanes and overtake slower traffic, but her confidence would not have extended to breaking her journey for a cup of tea or the pee which she was beginning to crave. The suggested stay at a hotel was also out of the question. She might never be able to set off again in the morning, added to which she had little money on her and no cheque book or credit card. Fortunately, Darryl had filled up just before they arrived at the venue. She whiled away the time by planning her moves for when she arrived at Darryl's door.

She seemed to be getting along better now. During her ruminations, the traffic had largely died away and she had three lanes of motorway all to herself. Perhaps she could speed up a little more. She took her eyes off the road for the first time and glanced down at the speedometer. It took several seconds for the reading to register in her tired mind. 115 mph! She closed the throttle gently until she was back within the legal limit and hoped to God that she hadn't wandered through any speed cameras.

The adrenalin surge dissipated. It had been a long day with an excess of fresh air. The demands of riding the motorbike kept her from falling asleep but she lapsed into an almost hypnotic trance. Once, her speed picked up again and she nearly ran into the back of a lorry. She gave herself a good talking to and concentrated on planning for her arrival at home.

There was only one unresolved flaw in her forward planning by the time she left the motorway again. She knew the streets well enough by now to be able to pick a route which avoided most of the traffic lights; the inescapable few were radar controlled so that the lights changed in her favour. She was within a quarter-mile of home when a police car overtook her and waved her down.

For an awful moment, Polly was afraid that she would never remember the whereabouts of the brakes, clutch and gears. With a conscious effort she commanded her memory to work. Feeling sick, Polly slowed, found neutral and came to a halt. As long as she kept the machine near vertical she found that she could hold it in balance but she knew that once she let it start to lean, disaster would follow.

A uniformed officer got out of the car and approached. Polly switched off the engine and pushed up her visor. "Good-evening," she said. "Did I do something wrong?"

"Good Lord! It's a woman!" said the officer. He coughed apologetically. "I beg your pardon, but we don't often get a . . . a lady riding through the streets at such an hour. There was an incident near here and we were told to keep an eye out for anything unusual."

"What sort of incident?"

"Screams were heard, that's all I've been told. No, madam, you did nothing wrong. But you were going remarkably slowly; that usually means a driver who's been drinking. Have you been drinking?"

"Only tea," Polly said.

"Would you mind removing the helmet?"

Polly did so. The officer sniffed and seemed to be reassured. "Is this your motorcycle, madam?" he asked.

Polly guessed that they had already checked the registration over the radio. "It belongs to Darryl Davidson," she said. "I've been staying with him."

"The wrestler, would that be?" The policeman seemed mildly amused by this evidence of human frailty.

"Yes. He was injured in the ring this evening. He asked me to fetch his bike home for him."

"A bit heavy for you, isn't it?"

"That's why I was going slow. Would you like to ride it the rest of the way for me?"

He shook his head, smiling. "May I see your driving licence?"

That was the dreaded question. "Help me balance this great brute?" she said. The officer gripped the handlebar while she removed her gloves and dug out her mother's purse. She extracted the driving licence. At the same time, she partly solved the last of her problems by transferring the key of the house door to Darryl's coat pocket. She held her breath. It still might be all right. Her mother had been driving for years and had steadfastly refused to have any permitted categories removed from her licence. The only snag was . . .

"That's all right, madam," said the officer. He returned the licence. "Do you have far to go?

"Just up the road."

"Ride carefully."

"I will, believe me." It occurred to Polly that she might ask the officers to come and help her get the motorbike up the steps, but she decided not to push her luck. She resumed her helmet, managed to re-start the engine, engaged a gear and pulled gently away. The officer stepped back and watched her go. Polly did not know whether to feel relieved or insulted that the policeman had accepted the date of birth coded into the licence number as being credible. It only went to show, she thought, that the day's tribulations had put years on her.

Her mouth had gone dry – not because of the trial just past, but for the test still to come. She was almost home. She went over the drill in her mind, but Darryl's house was reached so quickly that she was doing it as soon as thinking it. Down to bottom gear. Look up and down the street. Make the turn without quite laying the bike down. Cross the street at right-angles. Crawl to the bottom of the shallow steps as slowly as she could balance. Then give it some throttle, slip the clutch, bump up the steps and onto the plat. At the critical moment, clutch and brake. She thumped the wheel into the door but thought that she might not have done any damage. She fished the key out of her right-hand pocket and just managed to reach the lock. The door swung open. Last lap. She settled back into the saddle and bumped up the final step into the hall, stopping the engine and parking beside the scooter. With a last, great effort, she heaved the machine onto its stand. Made it! She was suddenly conscious of her entire body being bathed in sweat under the leathers and she was ravenously hungry. She dashed for Darryl's bathroom, leaving behind her a trail of clothing.

At last she could spare some concentration from directing and controlling the monster. While she had juggled the key at the front door she had been aware of something in the shadows beside the doorway, but beyond deciding that it had neither menace nor relevance to her immediate problem she had ignored and almost forgotten it. Now it returned to her mind. What had it been? A dozen possible interpretations of her recorded impression flitted past, each more improbable than its predecessor.

Well, there was one way to settle it. When her bladder was at last empty, she went back to the still open front door, gathering discarded garments as she went, and looked outside. A figure was squatting beside the door, curled up tightly into a foetal position.

"What the hell are you doing here?" she asked it. Slowly, Diana raised her head a few inches and cocked one eye in Polly's direction. Then she lowered her head again.

"Suit yourself," Polly said. "Stay there as long as you like. Just don't make a mess." She turned back.

"Wait. Please. Don't leave me."

The words were only a whisper. A whisper is a poor medium for conveying emotion, yet Polly knew from the tone rather than the content that the other woman was desperate. A shiver crept up her back. She looked around carefully in case this were a trap but there was nobody else to be seen. "What on earth's the matter? Have you had an accident?"

"It wasn't an accident."

Polly stopped herself from asking whether she'd been thumped for pinching somebody else's purse. "Why did you come here?"

"I couldn't think of anywhere else to go. This was my home once. Please, can I come in? Just for a little while?"

Polly was on the point of asking her where she got off, demanding hospitality after all that had gone before, but at that moment Diana raised her head. Even in the poor light of a distant street lamp, Polly could see that the other woman's face was bloodied. The blood looked jet black in the yellow light.

Polly turned back into the hall and dumped her armful of garments over the scooter. When she tried to help her to her feet it was evident that Diana's body troubled her most. She could not straighten herself and could walk only with difficulty, bent half double and mewing like a kitten.

Polly, still half suspecting a trap, was careful to push the front door closed behind them. Diana could never have managed the stairs. Polly was too tired to carry her and was becoming painfully aware of her bruised knee. She managed to support the other as they moved in a tragi-comic dance to Darryl's door and into his flat, locking and bolting the door behind them. She lowered Diana onto Darryl's bed.

In the stronger light she could see that Diana's mouth was badly swollen and there was bleeding from her mouth and nose. Close examination suggested that the blood could be accounted for by superficial damage and did not necessarily indicate serious internal injuries. But before helping the other woman she had to help herself. Coming into the warm house from the biting air, during the moments that it had taken her to get rid of her surplus clothing her body temperature had shot up. Suddenly she knew what hell must be like. She washed quickly in cold water, which helped both to cool her and to wake her up. The hour was late and she had had a long and busy day. Hot sweet tea was the first priority for both of them. She put the kettle on.

Polly had read somewhere that cold rather than heat was the remedy for bruising. She found a basin, filled it with cold water, added ice cubes from Darryl's fridge and used his sponge to wipe away the blood. Diana, without quite uncurling, submitted like a child, only flinching once or twice, but her swollen mouth was unsteady and her tears mingled with the water. Two of her front teeth were broken.

The kettle came to the boil. Polly made a pot of tea. She steeled herself to investigate further. Nothing would have surprised her. "Straighten up and lean back," she told Diana.

"I can't."

"That's what I thought. I'm going to call a doctor."

"No." For the first time, Diana's voice was raised almost to normal. "No. I'll be all right. I don't want any doctors."

"Why not?"

"I just don't."

"Well, straighten up and let's have a look at you."

Groaning, Diana managed to do as she was told. She was wearing trousers and a blouse under her coat, so that Polly had no difficulty opening her clothes. She would not have been surprised to find evidence of a knife or even a bullet but, to Polly's great relief, there was no puncture-wound. Bruising was already developing over Diana's stomach and ribs and when she leaned forward again Polly saw that her back was similarly battered. The marks looked like punches rather than kicks, but Polly, sensible of her own ignorance, could not be sure.

Polly was uncertain whether aspirin or paracetamol was to be preferred if there was internal damage, so she decided to administer two of each from Darryl's small stock. Darryl did not seem to possess a hot-water bottle so she put the remaining ice cubes into a freezer-bag and gave them to Diana to hold on her mouth. Ignoring the other's complaints, which were becoming peevish rather than agonised, she pulled Diana to her feet, stripped off the rest of her clothes and stretched her out on the bed. There were a few more bruises on the arms and legs, but in the main the damage was much as she had already seen. There was no blood. Polly searched her mind for the crumbs of medical and first aid knowledge that had settled there over the years. "Does it hurt you to breathe?" she asked.

"Not really." Diana seemed surprised to find that there was something that did not pain her.

"I don't know what else I can do," Polly said. "I'd dunk you in a bath of ice-water, only you'd get hypothermia. At least you're not bleeding anywhere external."

"That's good, as far as it goes," Diana murmured apathetically.

Polly closed her mind to thoughts of internal bleeding. She poured tea into two mugs and gave one to Diana. "Sit up and drink this. Then, if I get you dressed again and call a taxi, could you manage for yourself?"

Diana jerked awake and became suddenly more lucid. "I can't go home. They'd know where to find me."

"Who would?"

"Ronald Dent and his thugs."

"It seems to me," Polly said, "that they've already done whatever they were going to do to you. Can't your friend Hugo Tyrone look after you?"

Diana gave a hollow laugh. "Hugo? He could never stand up to Ronnie Dent, he's not the physical type. Anyway, he's on a flight to New York. And you don't know what else they'd do." She sniffed wetly and her voice cracked. "They think I'm Daphne and nothing I said seemed to get them away from the idea. You know what I'm talking about?"

Polly thought quickly. *Should* she know who Daphne was? "It was on the radio," she said. She was pleased to find that she was developing the knack of screening her words.

"You see, I'm the only woman they could think of who might have known enough to give the police what they've got. There must be another one somewhere but they only had me. Or maybe there's a man using the name Daphne. Why not?"

"Could be," said Polly. If they did this to the wrong woman, what wouldn't they do to the right one?

Diana yawned suddenly. Shock and the analgesics were catching up with her. Polly took a long drink of her own tea. It gained her a moment for thought. She had nearly said, *But you're not Daphne.* She would have to guard her tongue even more carefully. "You're sure you're not Daphne?" she asked carefully.

Diana shivered. "I wouldn't bloody dare," she said. "I don't know who she is, but she's got my vote. Or he has."

"You should go to the police. They could protect you."

"You've got to be joking. They'd either keep me in protective custody or turn me out to get beaten up again."

"You could end up being looked after in hospital with a guard beside your bed."

"And I might win the lottery. Please, I'm scared. Couldn't I stay here, just for the night?"

"We both know what happened last time you were here," Polly said sternly.

Diana covered her face. "There wouldn't be anything like that, on my mother's grave. On *my* grave."

"I suppose you'll have to stay," Polly said reluctantly. "But if there's any bloody nonsense, what Ronald Dent and his boys gave you tonight will just be a warm-up for the main event. And if there's any blood in your urine, into hospital you go anyway."

There was no answer except for a light snore. Diana was sound asleep. Polly rolled her over and tucked her in. She cooked and ate a quick meal of bacon and eggs. While she performed her own ablutions, she caught sight of herself in the mirror. No wonder, she thought, that the policeman had accepted the birth date on the driving licence. Between exhaustion and a total lack of makeup, and with her hair flattened by the helmet, she looked older than her mother had ever allowed herself to look. Oh well, tomorrow would be another day and if she went on saving up she might be able to afford a facelift. She considered sleepily what to do next. While Diana was here, calling the police would be a mistake.

Later, perhaps.

Before crawling into Darryl's bed beside Diana, she checked the locks and bolts. Darryl had a pair of Indian clubs, for exercising at home. Polly stood them beside the bed. They would not be such good weapons as pick-handles or baseball bats, but they might be better for one-handed swinging and if somebody came calling in the night they would have to do.

There were no alarms in the night. Polly, exhausted by her experiences and the overdose of fresh air, slept like a hibernating tortoise and woke suddenly in the late morning, still half-fuddled. When she had managed to

109

recall why she was in Darryl's room again, she would not have been surprised to find that Diana had vanished, taking with her any portable valuables that she could put her hand on. But no. There was a warm and heavy shape beside her in the bed and when she turned back the bedclothes to get out she was greeted by a long and mournful groan.

"How are you this morning?" she asked.

"Not up to answering bloody silly questions." The answer came from somewhere under the bedclothes.

Polly was in no mood to suffer petulance from somebody who had never done her any favours. "If you're going to be like that," she said, "you can get dressed and go."

The blonde head, which was showing its dark roots, emerged in a hurry. Diana seemed ready to start snivelling again. Her voice was squeaky with fear. "I'm sorry. Really I am. Let me stay, just a little longer. *Please*. I've nowhere to go and anyway I couldn't move."

"Well, mind your manners. Let's have a look at you." Polly pulled down the blankets. The bruising had developed in the night. Polly had seen similar injuries after a hard game of hockey, though never so many at the same time. They would mend, but in the meantime any movement would undoubtedly be painful. "Stay there and rest," Polly said. "Time is the healer. Could you manage some breakfast?"

"Oh God! I couldn't eat."

"Tea, then?"

"I think so, please."

Polly made tea, took a quick shower and ate her usual light breakfast while getting dressed. She was relieved to see that her face had regained its colour and texture and, with her hair brushed out, she could have passed for any age between eighteen and thirty. Diana managed to prop herself up and drink the heavily sweetened tea.

"I have to go out," Polly said. "Can you survive?"

"Just let me lie here and wait for Christmas. I should be able to move around by then."

"You'll be out of here long before then," Polly assured her. Diana must be on the mend already if she could make jokes, but Polly was satisfied that the other was not going anywhere in a hurry. In addition to her injuries, she was still too frightened.

"You're not going to tell anybody where I am?" Diana asked suddenly.

"Why would I? Is Ronald Dent offering a reward?"

Diana turned white. "Nothing like that," she said.

"Why are you still afraid? They've done what they were going to do and they've let you go."

"If the police have found out any more, Ronnie Dent may think it came from me." Diana forced herself to take an unemotional look at the facts. "Maybe you're right," she said at last. "Maybe you're not as thick as you look and I'm being paranoid. But somebody said that when the whole world's against you, paranoia is only common sense."

"When the whole world's against you," Polly said, "winding your neck in and being polite to people is even more sensible."

"I suppose so. Would you fetch something from Hugo's flat for me? Please?"

"No, I bloody well wouldn't," Polly said. Apart from the fact that what she would be asked to fetch would probably include drugs, there was no knowing what else she might be walking into. "They may be watching it," she said, "and if I turned up to fetch your things they'd know where to look for you."

"That's true," said Diana. "I'm sorry I said you looked thick. You're not stupid at all."

Polly touched on a little makeup and rode the scooter to the gym. The cleaning ladies were still at work. She set to, sorting out the muddle that Slasher had made of the paperwork. When the phone rang some time later, it was Darryl from his hospital bed. "I'll be quick," he said. "The price of calls from here is a rip-off. You got my bike back safely?"

"Hardly hit a thing," Polly said.

Darryl rightly assumed that she was joking. "That's great. Everything okay at the gym?"

"The cleaners want to be paid. How much do I give them? But first tell me how you are."

"It's a simple fracture," he said. "They're letting me out tomorrow, with a cast and crutches. I'll come by train and get a taxi from the station."

"Let me know your time of arrival and I'll meet you with the taxi."

"No need to pay for a taxi both ways."

"I want to talk to you on the way home."

Rather than prolong an expensive call, Darryl finished quickly and hung up. Polly paid the cleaners and opened the gym for the afternoon.

The death of Patrick Mahon had been superseded by a scandal involving two politicians, a call-girl and funds collected for charity and that story was, for the moment, old news. There was no mention of it on Polly's radio, but one of the boxers had seen Harry Hains in the street. "He must have got bail," he said.

A Running Jump

"Can you get bail on a murder charge?" Polly asked.

"They probably reduced it to manslaughter seeing as it couldn't have been done on purpose," Slasher said. "Anyway, he won't dare show his face here. Too many of us who remember Mr Mahon digging us out of trouble." He smiled reminiscently. "He was good that way, was Mr Mahon. He was a tiger for discipline but when there was trouble he'd fight for his babies. That's what he called us, his babies. But only when there was trouble. The rest of the time, you'd hardly believe what he called us. Words I still don't understand, mostly."

The news of Darryl's injury had already spread over the wrestler's grapevine. The general feeling was that Frankie Delrose would run out of opponents unless he mended his ways. A remarkable number of the customers had seen Polly's intervention in the ring on television, because an excerpt from the recording had been used as an amusing tailpiece to the TV news, and they gave ever more glowing accounts to those who had not. One of the morning papers had a photograph obviously pirated from the television, with the headline, *Mystery teenager KOs champ.* Polly found herself in the position of a heroine. She was also appointed treasurer of the Darryl Davidson benefit fund and a worthy start was made on the spot. The wrestlers present promised to spread the word and raise contributions at future venues. Polly issued herself with a locker in order to keep the money quite separate from the gym funds.

When Polly got home later in the evening, Diana was still in bed and feeling sorry for herself. The bruising was now in technicolor and the swelling seemed to be at its worst, but her morale had hit a low which, Polly judged, might have been due to withdrawal from drugs as much as to fear and her aches and pains. But she managed to take a boiled egg, tea and toast, which Polly assumed to be a small sign of recovery.

"Why would they think that you were Daphne?" she asked suddenly.

"I don't want to talk about it," Diana said and buried her head under the bedclothes.

Polly settled down to watch Darryl's television. She was in time to see a replay of her valiant attack on Frankie Delrose. She had certainly caught him a mighty wallop. Now that she knew Frankie, she would have felt rather sorry for him but for the fact that he had injured Darryl. She herself didn't look too bad. But she did wish that she had had her hair done.

Seven

Polly had an early night. For this she was later to be very thankful, because her sleep was interrupted. During the small hours she was awoken by a knocking at the front door. She waited, clinging to sleep for comfort and hoping without much hope that one of the other tenants might be expecting a visitor or an urgent parcel and would rush to the door. But there was no sound except for resumed hammering. Beside her, Diana slept like the dead. The knocking continued, more demanding than ever. Polly got out of bed, yawning and muttering under her breath, and peeped through the curtains. The form of a policeman was discernible on the step outside.

She opened the window an inch or two and spoke. "What is it?"

The policeman shone his torch in her direction. "Is Mr Davidson there?"

Polly was only wearing a T-shirt. She pulled the curtain around her legs. "He's in hospital."

"Is there any other keyholder for his gymnasium?"

"Me, I suppose," Polly admitted reluctantly.

"Somebody's been seen on the roof. We think that they escaped over the back walls. But you'd better open up for us. Can you come?"

Stifling her annoyance, Polly splashed cold water on her face, threw on some clothes and hunted for the keys to the gym. She made the officer show his identification before she took the chain off the door. Anyone, she told him, could have attached a chequered band to a chauffeur's cap. The constable said that she was very wise. Polly managed a brief doze in the police car. At the gym, she put up all the lights. The place looked no more bare than it usually did. "Nothing seems to have been disturbed," she said.

The other constable, who had driven the police car, asked, "Is there anything valuable here?" He sounded doubtful.

"There a little money in the lockers," Polly said, "but not a lot and they don't seem to have been touched. Some of the gear would be expensive to replace but I can't think that anyone would want to steal a punch-bag or a wrestling mat, or even an exercise machine."

The first constable had prowled around, looking for possible points of entry. "There aren't any windows," he said, "and the rooflights have solid-looking grilles over them. I don't think the visitor got inside."

"Better make sure," said his partner. The two men prowled around the building, shining their torches into likely and unlikely hiding places for an intruder and even up into the dusty interstices of the roof-space.

"If he's here," Polly said wearily, "he must have slipped in through the keyhole and he's hiding inside a boxing glove." That view was generally accepted. The officers returned Polly to the house, promising to keep a regular eye on the gym for the remainder of their shift. Polly went back to bed.

She was woken again, it seemed only minutes later,

by Darryl's phonecall. He would be arriving by train late in the morning.

Polly made tea and put a mug beside Diana. She shook the other's shoulder and made sure that the tea had been seen and recognised. Her consideration was rewarded only with a grunt. "What seems to be missing," Polly said, "are just two little words." Diana said two little words. "Not those two little words," said Polly sternly. "The ones I had in mind were 'Thank' followed by 'you'. Try them. They won't hurt your mouth any more than it's been hurt already."

There was an inarticulate mumbling from under the bedclothes. Charitably putting Diana's bad temper down to withdrawal symptoms, Polly decided to interpret the mumbling as an expression of gratitude. "You'll have to move upstairs," she said.

"I couldn't walk."

Polly yawned and blinked. She was in no mood to stand any nonsense, especially from someone who had enjoyed an uninterrupted sleep. "It's that or find yourself standing on the doorstep in your birthday suit. You may be older than I am, but I can still handle you. Darryl's on his way home and I want to have his rooms ready for him. I'll give you some breakfast first. What do you fancy?"

Diana, chastened, opted for cereal as well as a boiled egg. She got out of bed and put on Darryl's gown to eat it. During the few moments of nudity, Polly had time to see that the bruises on Diana's body, like those on her face, were changing colour, fading from blue to purple and from purple to a greenish yellow. Definitely on the mend, Polly decided.

117

She fed them both and then shook off the last vestiges of sleep and switched into her hyperactive mode. She helped Diana into a hot bath, left her the radio for company and set about Darryl's two rooms. When all was ready for the arrival of another invalid, she helped Diana, wrinkled, pink and very clean, out of the bath, stuffed her into one of Darryl's shirts and led her up to what had once been her own room. Pocketing her cash, cheque book and watch, Polly made a quick dash to the shops and stowed away some essential provisions.

On the way out of the house she almost bumped into the frail figure of Mr Shanks, the elderly antique dealer. He paused for a moment of polite chat.

"Did you know Mr Mahon?" Polly asked on impulse. "The man who was killed last week?"

Mr Shanks nodded gravely. "I never met him. I knew *of* him, of course. His vase was well known to the trade. It seems to have been looted around the time of the burning of the Summer Palace although, of course, the vase would already have been more than five hundred years old even then. I've never been able to understand how that particular act of mass vandalism ever came to pass," he added irritably.

"It was at the time of the Taiping rebellion," Polly said. "There was a diplomatic mission of some sort and the Chinese took some British prisoners and executed them. The burning was a reprisal."

"A young lady of education," Mr Shanks remarked. "I suppose the vase will pass into the hands of some unscrupulous collector, probably in America or Japan, and not be seen again. A pity. It dates from the first of the Ming emperors. I forget his name. Do you, perhaps . . . ?"

118

Polly had had the names and dates of the Chinese emperors drummed into her. "Hengwu," she said.

Mr Shanks's eyes opened wide. "So it was! If you're looking for a job in antiques, let me know."

"I don't know anything about antiques!"

"But you have the ability to learn."

Polly filed the suggestion away for later consideration. "What would the vase be worth?" she asked.

Mr Shanks threw up his hands in despair. "Who can say? It was one of a kind. The only similar example, which is smaller and has been repaired, was auctioned recently. It made half a million pounds. The one we're talking about would make twice that on the open market. Between unscrupulous collectors . . . Well, if Heindrickson's client and, say, Elvyn Frascati of New York were bidding against each other, even the sky might not be the limit." He sighed. "That would be a sale worth handling. A man could retire after a sale like that."

Polly made suitably respectful noises and took her leave. She still had time in hand, so to pander to Darryl's compulsive thrift – an attitude with which she had some qualified sympathy – she walked. The streets around the railway station, which had seemed so ominous in darkness, were now cheerful and friendly. The train was on time. She found herself pleased and relieved to see Darryl's muscular form and friendly grin come through the barrier. He was swinging along confidently between a pair of National Health crutches. Polly noticed that one trouser-leg had been slit up the seam to allow for the plaster cast and had been re-fastened with surgical tape.

"I can't spare a hand from these things yet for a polite

119

handshake," he said, "so you'll have to make do with a kiss instead." He bent forward. Polly offered him her cheek but he kissed her gently on the lips.

Polly decided not to make any overt comparison between his kiss and that of Frankie Delrose. "Here! What's all this?" she said. "I thought you didn't like girls."

"I never said I didn't like them. Or if I did I could make an exception. It's great to see you. The maiden who galloped to the knight's rescue. My gallant Amazon! My Valkyrie!" Polly laughed, embarrassment gone. Of course, she supposed, his kisses would be as between sisters.

Outside the station there was a queue for taxis. Polly drew Darryl to the head of the queue. "This gentleman can't stand for long," she said. "Would anybody object if he took the next cab to come along?" Darryl's cast and his crutches were in plain view. Nobody objected aloud. Seconds later, a taxi carried them off.

"You've got some brass neck," Darryl said. "What happened to the taxi you came in?"

"I walked. I thought you probably couldn't afford to pay for a taxi both ways—"

"Right on!"

"—seeing that you owe me for riding your bike all the way back – which would have cost you a bomb if you'd had to send it by carrier – and looking after the gym yesterday and cleaning it, laying in a supply of food for you and being called out in the night because somebody thought they saw a man on the roof."

"But I shan't be wrestling for God knows how long," Darryl said plaintively. "When my leg's mended I'll still have to get my fitness back. I shan't be earning."

A Running Jump

"You'll have the gym money coming in and the rent from your tenants—"

"And mortgages to pay on both of them, and Council Tax. And you wouldn't believe what the gym costs to heat."

"The other wrestlers really are getting up a subscription for you and there's already money in the kitty. I told them that you were losing money on the gym and only kept it on for their benefits. They don't know that you own the house."

Darryl whistled. "You've not just got brass neck, you've got a bloody nerve. And you're right," he said humbly. "I do owe you. Where are we going? The carvery? I'll buy you lunch."

"We're going home," Polly told him. "Lunch comes cheaper there."

She had intended to warn Darryl about Diana while they were in the taxi, but the driver would have heard every word and might have talked. She waited until the taxi set them down. Darryl paid the driver with hardly a grumble and managed to lever himself up the steps. At the door to his own flat, he stopped and sniffed. "The place smells different," he said.

"It smells clean," Polly told him.

As soon as he was seated comfortably with his crutches leaning against the table, Polly set about making a salad while she told him about the arrival of Diana. She was putting cold, sliced meat and mustard on the table when she finished. She grated cheese over the salad and put out a bowl of fruit.

"That's why the room smells different," Darryl said. "You've both been sleeping here. Diana always did use too much scent. She's upstairs now?"

121

"Yes."

"She's got a bigger bloody nerve than you have, and that's really saying something. Coming here for help after I kicked her out and you had to fight her to get your money back!" Frowning, Darryl made himself a sandwich with the meat and some fresh, wholegrain bread. "What would have given anyone the idea that she was Daphne? Similarity of the names?"

"That's a good question," said Polly. "I've been asking myself the same thing. You may be right. I'm beginning to have my own ideas, but they're too vague to talk about just yet."

Polly took a tray up to the other invalid. She was thanked for it. "I nearly dropped the tray," she told Darryl later. "She must be getting over the shock. Only she's having nightmares and throwing herself around in the bed. It's like sleeping with a dervish or something."

"Can't you get rid of her now?"

Polly made a face. "She's still terrified and she doesn't have anywhere else to go. I couldn't do that to her. Not just yet."

"Whatever you say. This is good food. I'll have to come to this restaurant more often."

"It's healthy food," Polly pointed out. "But you just like it because it's cheap."

Darryl settled down to live the life of an invalid, watching television and being waited on. That lasted less than an hour. When Polly got ready to go and open the gym, he struggled to his feet. "Take the scooter out," he said, and then, "Hang on. I'm coming with you."

"Darryl, you *can't!*"

"How much do you bet?"

Polly walked the scooter down the steps. Darryl, his helmet already on his head, followed her down. With some difficulty, he swung his cast over the pillion and settled his weight behind Polly, holding her clumsily. The crutches were pointing skyward and his cast was against her left thigh. "Get going," he said. "This is a bit of a strain."

Polly had serious doubts. The last thing she wanted was to be stopped by the police and to have her mother's driving licence scrutinised during daylight hours. In the event, the scooter still balanced well. They attracted a few amused glances but no other attention.

Darryl was pleased to approve Polly's efforts as clerk, book-keeper, secretary and receptionist. He wrote her out a cheque for a sum which was neither lordly nor miserly but, Polly admitted to herself, appropriate. "You did that without flinching," Polly said. "You must be turning normal."

Darryl was frank. "When I was a kid, I saw my father go bust," he said. "And I saw the effect it had on my parents. I think it killed my dad in the end. I made up my mind that it was never going to happen to me. So ever after, I've been putting my money away. It's become a habit that's hard to break."

"You were putting it away for a rainy day and it's raining now."

"That's what I'm telling myself." Darryl frowned at an innocent calendar. "Now that this has happened I've got to recognise that I'm facing a setback and setbacks can come any time that luck lets you down. It'll make a dent in my savings, but that's what they're for. This, as you tell me, is the proverbial rainy day, not the end of the world."

"Keep telling yourself that," Polly told him. "I'll help you to keep a sense of proportion."

She spoke lightly but Darryl nodded seriously. "That's what I need," he said. "A sense of proportion. I suppose I'm middle-of-the-road comfortable, but most of the time I feel either rich or, more often, bankrupt."

One of the first clients to arrive, a fellow wrestler, brought a copy of *The Mail* with its own version of the story. On the back page, a headline screamed MYSTERY GIRL FELLS FRANKIE DELROSE. There were photographs, this time taken by an amateur photographer near the ringside. In one, she was kneeling beside Darryl and facing the camera and Polly was horrified to see that she was clearly recognisable and that her hair was seen to be quite out of control. At least in the television pictures it had been blurred by motion. The only comfort was that if there was one paper in the world that her mother would never read it would be *The Mail*.

"At the hospital," Darryl said, "I had reporters the way another patient had nits. I didn't tell them anything about you. I said that my usual second couldn't be there and I asked a girl who was in a seat beside my corner to hand me my towel and water bottle between rounds. I said that I wished I knew who she was because I wanted to thank her for getting Frankie off me. I don't suppose they believed me."

"What did you say about Frankie?" asked the wrestler.

Darryl winked. "The usual. Didn't realise how much damage he'd done. Got a bit carried away. That sort of thing. It's all very well having pretend feuds," Darryl explained to Polly. "They can be good publicity. But when you let real feuds get out of proportion, fans may come to watch the mayhem but sooner or later somebody gets badly hurt."

"Somebody did get hurt," Polly pointed out.

"There's worse things than a simple fracture in the leg," Darryl said.

"I met Frankie Delrose in the hall after they took you away. He didn't seem to mind being kicked in the head at all."

"Happens all the time," the other wrestler said. "He wouldn't mind as long as it was a girl."

"I didn't exactly fancy him," Polly said, choosing her words with care. "But he didn't seem like a bad sort of person. If any reporter comes nosing around here," she told the other wrestler, "do something nasty to them."

"Anything, just as long as you don't treat me the way you did Frankie Delrose. I bet his head hasn't stopped throbbing yet." Grinning, he pretended to duck out of the way of a blow. "Why don't you want any publicity? Most girls would be all out for the glory."

"I just don't, Polly said. She was keeping a secret hugged to her bosom. That day was her eighteenth birthday, bringing with it several changes to her legal status. She would dearly have loved to celebrate it with Darryl. But she had already shattered a number of laws and she had a strong suspicion that her mother could easily resume legal control of her, nor did she intend to let Darryl know just how young she was.

Darryl had still not acquired a taste for idleness, or else he had suffered an excess of it in the hospital. One leg might be incapacitated but he could still keep the remainder of his body fit. He stripped to the waist and

125

started working out on those machines which exercised the arms and upper body. Later, he sent Polly out for a strap which enabled him to operate an exercise bicycle with his undamaged leg. Polly, who had been accustomed to school games, was feeling the lack of exercise and due to the unaccustomed diet she had put on a few unwelcome ounces. Between times, she began to do a little work on the easier machines. She decided to buy herself a sweatsuit out of Darryl's cheque.

They dined later, on more cold meat and salad which Polly had brought from the house. Polly felt a faint twinge of conscience because nobody was looking after Diana but, as Darryl said, "What did she ever do for you?"

"Not a lot. But Ronald Dent may be on the point of finding her."

"I don't see how. You're more likely to lead him to her if you fuss over her. That's if he wants her at all. I don't see why he would. He's already done her over."

Polly had been giving that aspect some more thought. "Diana keeps talking about Ronnie Dent," she said. "She says that her Hugo was away on a flight. But I think it may have been the boyfriend who did her over. That would be one reason she doesn't want to go back to his flat. She's still worried about Dent because he hasn't had his go at her yet."

"Makes sense," Darryl admitted.

During the evening, they were interrupted by a uniformed constable. Darryl received him in the office and called Polly in a minute later.

"It's about Mr Mahon's death," Darryl said, looking

126

Polly in the eye. "Did you take any phone messages for Harry Hains?"

Truth was safest. "Over the phone? Only one."

"There were others?" the constable asked keenly. Polly guessed that he was out to impress his superiors.

"Darryl – Mr Davidson here – took another one and asked me to give the message to Mr Hains."

"I took about half a dozen over a period of a week," Darryl said. The text of the messages, as nearly as they could remember them, were quoted and written down.

"Could you describe the voice?"

"*I* couldn't," Polly said.

"It was just a voice," Darryl said. "A man's voice. No higher or deeper than average. Slightly nasal, perhaps."

"Accent?"

"I didn't notice any."

"Very faint," Polly said, suddenly remembering. "But it was there. English rural, but not from right here. And I think he was speaking from a call box."

The constable frowned. "You don't get to hear the coins drop or somebody pressing Button A any more."

"There was a lot of traffic noise," Polly said. "It was very noticeable. I thought at the time that it would have to be a call box, or possibly a mobile, not somebody's house. Not unless they were using the phone near an open window."

"I noticed it too, now you come to remind me," said Darryl.

"That explains why they haven't been able to trace the call," said the constable. "But that's the way it goes. My instructions are to ask you both kindly to come to

127

the incident room, one at a time, and listen to tapes. It won't take minutes."

Darryl went first, by police car. When he returned, the same constable was with him and watching him, but his face was carefully blank. Polly in her turn was conveyed to the incident room, a borrowed classroom in a nearby school. The big room had clearly been busy during the day, but so late in the evening was occupied only by a figure guarding the telephone and another doing something with a desktop computer. A corner had been screened off for interviews and a man in plain clothes, who introduced himself as DS Williams, was brooding over two large tape recorders.

DS Williams had a fatherly manner. "There's nothing to be nervous about," he said. "I just want you to listen to these voices and tell me if you recognise any of them."

"I only heard the voice once," Polly said. "You're not taping me, are you?" She tried to change the pitch of her voice very slightly and reverted to her more up-market accent, in case the Sergeant Something who had taken Daphne's message should hear her.

"Would you mind?"

"I'd rather you didn't. I get nervous."

"All right. And once may prove to have been enough." He stopped one tape recorder and started the other. Six different voices repeated the same words, evidently a few lines from the pages of a novel. Polly noticed that one of the characters was a Harry and that the word 'rains' occurred. When the voices finished, he said, "Well?"

"My best guess would be Number Four," Polly said, "but I couldn't swear to it. They all sounded similar."

"Nothing to be sorry about," DS Williams said

cheerfully. "Mr Davidson said the same. We win some and lose some."

Polly decided that a little dissimulation might not go amiss. "What's the significance of those messages?" she asked. "Why does anyone care who phoned Mr Hains about his job in Russia?"

The Detective Sergeant seemed quite willing to pass a little of his evening duty in chatting with a young lady. "There wasn't any job in Russia," he said. "On the other hand, the men who made the attack which led to Mr Mahon's death would have wanted to choose an ideal night, when they wouldn't be heard by the neighbour below and they wouldn't meet anyone on the stairs who might remember them later. The messages may have been a discreet way of letting him know whether the job was on or not."

"How interesting!" Polly said.

The constable delivered her back to the gym. "I didn't give anything away," she told Darryl.

They closed the gym a little early and Darryl waited while Polly did the essential cleaning. They checked the rooflights, looked in every nook and corner and locked the heavy doors carefully.

The night was dark and the streets were slick with dew but they made the journey safely. Darryl dismounted at the bottom of the steps. "Come out again when you've put the scooter away," he said. "We'll have a drink in the casino. My round."

"Your treat at last?" Polly asked happily. "How did you know it was my birthday?"

"Is it?"

"I was joking," Polly explained, hiding her smile. "If

129

we're going to the casino I want a minute or two to change."

Darryl threw up his hands and nearly fell. "When a woman says that, she means an hour or two," he said.

"When I say it, I mean a minute or two," Polly retorted. "Maybe three. But I'd better shoot some soup into our guest. You hobble over and I'll join you. Twenty minutes maximum."

She found Diana peevish with hunger and heated a quick meal of convenience foods while she washed and changed into her trouser suit. She ran a comb through her hair, looked in the mirror and decided that she could get by with only a fleeting touch of makeup.

Within the promised twenty minutes, she was in the basement bar. They were earlier than usual and the bar was half full. One or two people, seeing Darryl and recognising her from her images in the media, smiled at her. With a sudden tilt of her stomach she noticed Ronald Dent at a table beside the bar, accompanied by a dyed redhead with a very low décolletage. Polly could almost see her nipples. She decided that the girl would be unwise to sneeze in company.

Darryl, at a corner table with a pint in front of him, had been joined by Mr Franklyn but the dapper manager lifted his rotund body out of the chair as she came up. "The local heroine," he said. "That clip of you saving your boyfriend's leg with a quick kick to his opponent's jaw is still being repeated. I'll have to hire you to help out with security." There were so many inaccuracies in the words that Polly did not know where to begin. She decided to let them all go and muttered some incoherent disclaimer.

Darryl produced his wallet. "Get yourself a drink from the bar," he said.

Mr Franklyn intervened. "It's on the house. What will you take? Only a shandy? I'll send it over."

When he was out of earshot, Polly asked, "What was Mr Dent talking about, the first time we were in here? Something about whether you'd thought something over."

"I don't know," Darryl said.

"You must know. You said that he'd asked you again. And you couldn't think something over without knowing what it was," Polly pointed out.

"Well, I don't. I told him I'd think it over rather than say 'no' to his face. He keeps asking me if I wouldn't like to earn some extra money on some of my trips. He wants me to carry something but I don't want any part of it. I'm as fond of money as the next man – all right, probably fonder – but not the sort of money that Ronald Dent hands out. That comes too expensive by half. He's a tricky sod. I'd probably deliver one parcel of dope or stolen goods and be in his clutches for ever after, that's the kind of way he works. He'd probably have me leaning on some poor bugger who owes him money or else my fingerprints would turn up on something lethal or stolen."

"You're quite right not to want any part of it," Polly said decisively. Looking around the room, she saw a face. Something stirred in her memory and in a few seconds she managed to isolate it. The man had been the fourth man with Dent, Hains and the American antique dealer, but he seemed to be keeping his distance from Dent now. He was being attentive instead to a well dressed, middle-aged woman. "Who's that man in the corner?" Polly asked.

131

Darryl looked. "No idea," he said. Without being obvious about it, Polly took several good looks at the man.

Mr Franklyn had spoken to the barmaid on his way out, but when that lady arrived she set down a pair of tall, thin glasses. "You'll get your shandy whenever you want it," she said. "But this is champagne, from Mr Dent over there."

For a moment Polly thought that it might be a macabre joke, a celebration of having penetrated Daphne's identity or a stirrup-cup for the grave. But then she glanced at Ronald Dent and saw that his harsh features were softened into something evidently intended as a friendly smile. He raised his glass to her. The redhead lifted her nose and pretended not to notice.

"He saw you on the telly on Saturday," said the barmaid. "He was full of it last night. He always hated that Frankie Delrose, he said, pulling all those dirty tricks." She set off back to the bar, wobbling on very high heels.

"Acknowledge it," Darryl said. "And smile." He raised his glass to Ronald Dent. Polly did the same.

Only a few minutes later, Dent and the redhead got to their feet. The girl headed in the direction of the Ladies', but Dent strolled to where Polly was sitting. Towering over them he brought with him his own atmosphere of rugged menace, but his mission was friendly. "Here's my new pin-up," he said, "and prettier than ever. That was a fantastic show you put up on Saturday. You'll have to come and work for me. I can always find work for a tough character."

"I'll bear it in mind," Polly said. She managed to smile.

"And get your boyfriend to bear my other proposition in mind," Dent said. "I can put some useful money his way."

"I'll make sure of it," Polly said vaguely. She decided that one secret might direct his attention away from another. "There are some people I don't want to find me," she said. "So, just in case the subject comes up while you're with any of your important friends, remember, you don't know who the girl is who kicked Frankie Delrose, or where she lives."

Dent laid a finger along his nose. He looked both amused and flattered. "Understood," he said.

"And your friend?"

"Trust me." Dent winked and turned away.

"As far as I could spit you," Darryl said softly to his receding back.

Polly raised her glass again and this time she took a sip. It was her first champagne and she didn't like it. The bubbles went up her nose.

When she could be sure that Darryl was asleep, Polly, still dressed, crept past his door and out into the street. It had turned into a miserable night. She hurried to the more remote of the two phone boxes and called the number of the incident room. Again the call was answered promptly although the voice sounded half asleep.

"This is Daphne."

The voice woke up suddenly. "Hey! The chief wants to talk to you."

"We don't all get what we want. Now listen. The man with Harry Hains was almost certainly a balding man, remaining hair sandy, between thirty and forty years old, prominent forehead, protruding teeth. Ears

133

also protruding, the left more than the right. Height about one metre eighty. Heavily built but not fat. He has a connection with Ronald Dent. Does that tell you anything?"

"The man I'm thinking of isn't one of Dent's usual cronies."

"Then he must be casual labour." Polly was wondering how far she could go. "They were seen looking at a picture of the Chinese pot together," she said. "But don't let them know that you know about that or you could put me on the spot. Good-night." She hung up on a sudden gabble and went back to bed. Diana was still restless.

Darryl had to admit that he had tried to do too much too soon. His leg was killing him next morning and he could move around only with difficulty. He refused to be seen by a doctor but readily agreed to spend a day or two at home with his leg up.

Despite the extra work, this suited Polly rather well. Diana was recovering, physically, and could now walk with care and cater for herself. She was still afraid to leave the house or even to go near the windows, but she could look after Darryl or go on her way. The choice, Polly told her, was hers.

"But I'm worse than he is," Diana moaned.

"You owe him for room and board," Polly retorted. "And you need the exercise. So get down there, keep him fed and watered and if he says 'Jump', you jump. Got it?"

Polly made sure that both her patients had adequate supplies of food and she left the house before her usual time. En route to the gym, she stopped off to buy herself the promised tracksuit. She was conscious of not having Darryl's reassuring protection with her and of having risked exposure as the informant. She rode the scooter carefully round the block and assured herself that there were no lurking figures to be seen before she stopped at the gym, took the scooter inside and barred the heavy door securely. She had been doing some heavy thinking and now she settled in Darryl's office and did some more.

She took a slip of paper out of her purse. On it was the number that Hugo Tyrone had been so anxious to recover. It was a long series of digits, beginning 001212. A search through Darryl's telephone directory revealed that 00 was the number of the international network, 1 was for the USA and 212 represented the Manhattan area of New York. That didn't take her much further. It could be the number of some girl. She looked at her watch, a cheap digital. One of these days she would be able to afford a better one. The time in New York would be early, but early birds should be stirring.

She pondered again and decided what to say in certain contingencies. Then she keyed the number. Remarkably soon, a phone rang in distant New York. It was picked up on the third ring. A voice which Polly was immediately sure belonged to that American status symbol, an English butler, intoned, "Mr Frascati's residence."

Polly put on her best American accent, the result of years of watching movies on television. "This is the Howmarket Gallery. We're just checking phone numbers. Is that the number for Mr Frascati, the porcelain collector?"

"That's so."

"His unlisted number?"

135

"Yes."

"Thank you. We'll get back to Mr Frascati later."
Polly terminated what had been a most informative
call. She had played a hunch and it had paid off. She
would have to try her luck at the casino while it was
running her way. Darryl could explain the intricacies of
the games.

Diana had been beaten up, probably by Tyrone but
possibly by Dent or his associates, on the assumption
that she was Daphne. But why would that assumption
have been made unless either she or Tyrone was in
the plot?

Ronald Dent had been dealing with a major collector
through the dealer Heindrickson. Presumably he had
been engaged to steal to order. They would need somebody to carry the goods across the Atlantic. Who more
suitable than Hugo Tyrone, an airline employee? Tyrone
had been carrying the unlisted number of another major
collector and had been very upset when he lost it. Perhaps
Dent was planning to double-cross Heindrickson and
his client.

On the other hand, perhaps Tyrone had been planning
to double-cross Dent, sell the goods to a different
collector and set himself up in comfort in Mexico
or Brazil. On reflection, that made a lot more sense.
Diana could have been beaten on behalf of Dent
in the hope of extracting Tyrone's present whereabouts, in which case her continued fear might derive
from the fact that she had, or might be thought to
have, heard from him subsequently. In fact, Dent
might think that Diana, as Daphne, had informed
to the police in order to get the avenging gangster
off her lover's track. That would certainly be another

136

explanation for her extreme reluctance to return to Tyrone's flat.

So the pot had already left the country. Or had it?

Almost certainly. But there was one other possibility. Tyrone might well be under suspicion. But was he guilty? There could have been another double-crosser.

Darryl did not seem to have kept a register of who had which locker, but there was a master-key in his desk. Polly set about going through the lockers one by one. At first the operation seemed profitless. She came across a great quantity of sporting garments and equipment and several unfamiliar items which she guessed to be jockstraps. She learned that two of the clients were addicted to pornographic magazines and another had transvestite tendencies. It was only when she came to the last locker but one that she found a neat stack of clothing in which she remembered seeing Harry Hains exercise. Hains, who had arrived late at night to collect, as he said, something from his locker.

He might not have been collecting but depositing something. His manner had been both nervous and furtive. Soon after that, he had been arrested and released on bail. He might well have feared reprisals if he had shown his face among the rougher former pupils of the late Mr Mahon. He was an acrobat. He could have been the night-time visitor on the roof, intending to get inside and recover it.

Polly felt down the back of the pile of clothes and found something hard and round, wrapped in what felt like newspaper.

Eight

V ery carefully, Polly lifted the bundle and carried it
through to Darryl's desk. She went back to close
the locker.

The vase, when unwrapped, did not look like a
million pounds – but then, she thought, a million
pounds probably did not look like a million pounds.
There would be a reward for its recovery, but how much?
Enough to ease Darryl's mind, enough to free her mother
from the need to batten on to lovers, enough to assure
herself a future? Probably not – even if the reward were
to come her way. Merely uncovering it in a locker which
the police would certainly have got round to searching in
time might not, could not be enough. Conscience fought
with cupidity but it was an unequal struggle. At eighteen,
fear of consequences is not the paramount emotion.

She knew what she was going to do. She wondered whether in the process she would be destroying
some valuable fingerprints, but if the criminals had
been too careful to leave prints around the death
scene they would hardly be likely to handle the loot
with ungloved hands. The pear-shaped vase, dark red
with faint decoration, went into one of the drawers of the desk but first she stroked the glaze. It
was almost glassy smooth but she thought that it

139

had just enough surface texture for what she had in mind.

She still had time to spare before the gym was due to open for business. She took out the scooter, locking up carefully and looking all round for lurking figures before setting off. She had noticed a shop selling artists' paraphernalia two streets away. She bought watercolour brushes and some materials.

Back at the gym she spread one of the newspapers over Darryl's desk and went to work. She gave the whole vase an all-over coat of off-white poster paint. She had difficulty at first making the water-based paint take to the porcelain glaze. Hoping that she was not doing terrible damage to a centuries-old patina, she washed the vase very gently and tried again with more success. When it was dry, she began to add a pattern.

She had never been more than average at Art, but any fool, she decided, could paint flowers. She dabbed in a blossom, clematis-style, on the shoulder of the vase. It looked passable, so she turned the vase and added another and, because the first two turned out to be not quite opposite each other, a third. It was a start. She added three more, below and between the others. In dark green, she touched in some twining stems and then a pattern of leaves. As soon as she abandoned any attempt at realism and instead portrayed her mental picture of the essence of floweriness, the effect was much more satisfying. Miss Morrison, her art teacher, she thought, would have been enraptured.

The first clients arrived before she was quite finished, but she opened up the gym. She was well liked by the men and she had to take some good-natured teasing. Her favourable comment on Frankie Delrose had done the rounds and somebody must have seen the kiss. She was the victim of endless humour on the subject but she just smiled and ignored it. She went back to work behind the closed door of the office. The men respected her privacy. She had begun to enjoy herself. Going slightly mad, she placed a disc of yellow at the centre of each flower, added veins to the leaves and dots of white to represent she knew not what. When she had drawn a shadow on each stem below the flower, she knew that she had done quite enough. Miss Morrison had been wont to say, in French, that, 'Better is the enemy of good'.

When all was hard she gave it a coat of shellac. She countered any tendency for the shellac to lift the poster paint by working gently and by repeating as closely as possible her earlier brushstrokes. She removed some files and put the vase in the deep bottom drawer of the desk and while it dried she changed into her new tracksuit.

In between running errands and seeing to the administration of the gym, she started a serious programme of working out, but the vase was always in her mind and she found time to give it a second all-over coat of shellac. She worked up a good sweat and took over the shower-room for a few minutes on the understanding that any man daring to intrude on her would be banned for a month. The threat sufficed. It seemed that none of the men felt that a month's ban would be a small price to pay for a glimpse of her naked loveliness. Polly was uncertain whether to feel relieved or insulted.

Between her artistic efforts, the new fitness regime and running the gym, the day slipped away. She was becoming practised at her gym-cleaning and doing the books and she made quick work of those duties. Darryl kept a powerful torch in his desk – so that he could be

141

sure to turn off all the machines in the event of a power failure, he had explained. Polly appropriated it.

She left for home after closing the gym and making a torchlight survey of the yard. The vase, wrapped in that day's newspapers, was in a polythene carrier-bag, slung over her shoulder haversack style on a skipping-rope borrowed from the gym. The original newspapers were disposed of in a nearby skip in case the dates should prove significant. The streets were slick with dew, so she rode very carefully. It would not have been a good occasion to fall off the scooter. All went well until she reached Darryl's front door. The skipping rope began to slip and as she reached for the lock the package made its way under her arm and clonked against the handlebar. Cursing ineffectually under her breath – the lack of good curses she considered to be a serious gap in her education – she pushed the package back into place only to have it move again and bump the doorpost as she and the scooter entered. In a fever of anxiety she parked the scooter and felt the package. She fully expected to find no more than a bag of shards but the vase felt intact.

She was anxious about her two patients after leaving them to their own devices for most of the day. But first she went into the garden. By torchlight she broke off several sprays from a cotoneaster shrub, scarlet with leaves and berries. Diana had probably gone through the contents of her room and would comment on any addition, so Polly went first into Darryl's apartment and set the vase and its contents on the mantelpiece. The red glaze showed through in occasional fine lines where the paint had been scratched, but that seemed only to enhance her design. The combination of colours, against a pale grey wallpaper, pleased her, but at the thought of all the happiness stored up inside she felt weak at the knees.

Darryl was lying on the couch, looking bored. "Where have you been all day?" he asked her.

The television was reproducing a panel game, with canned laughter. Polly turned it down. "If you want me to spend the afternoon and evening running your business for you," she retorted, "you must let me have the little that's left over for running my own errands. How's the leg?"

"It feels better if I keep my weight off it but I think it's mending."

"Are you starved?"

"Not really," he admitted. "You don't get very hungry, lying about like this. I could make good use of a cup of tea. But Diana came down twice and made us both something to eat."

"How did she seem?" Polly enquired. She had had a pub snack but that had been hours earlier. She set about making herself a quick sandwich.

"She can straighten up now and she doesn't look quite so much like the aftermath of something that scored about fifteen on the Richter scale. But she was still very sorry for herself and more scared than ever." He took notice of the fresh splash of colour on the mantel. "That's pretty."

"Family heirloom," Polly said. "Don't ever touch it." She would have to tell him some day but not until she was sure how he would react. She made a pot of tea and produced biscuits. They ate and drank in companionable silence.

Polly stirred at last. She rose and washed the two cups and a plate. "I'd better go and see to her. We'll

143

have to find somewhere else for her soon. I can't share a bed with her much longer. When she has nightmares she throws herself around. She'll punch me in the eye one of these nights."

"You could sleep down here," Darryl suggested. "Then, at a pinch, you could save me having to get out of bed and hop around the room if I need something. It's a much bigger bed than upstairs. And, honestly, I wouldn't lay a finger on you."

"I know you wouldn't," Polly said. The suggestion was attractive. She could escape from Diana and keep the vase under her own surveillance while being of possible service to Darryl and also remaining under his protection. If intruders should arrive with evil intent she would rather be with Darryl than Diana, even if the former had had both legs and an arm in casts.

"All right," she said. "Let's do that."

She went upstairs to check on Diana (who had fallen asleep with the radio playing and the lights on). She washed, cleaned her teeth and changed into the short nightdress which had been one of her purchases. Considering its skimpiness, she wondered if she hadn't been a little rash but decided that, with anyone of Darryl's persuasion, it was unlikely to matter.

Downstairs, Darryl had made similar preparations. He was lying almost on the extreme edge of the big bed. His pyjama jacket was brightly striped like that of a schoolboy. The only light was a bedside lamp, glowing gently and softening the shadows. By its light, Darryl looked very young. Polly slipped into the bed and settled on the opposite edge. Darryl switched off the lamp.

They lay in silence, warm under the covers. Polly had

occasionally imagined herself in bed with a man but it
had never been quite like this. With time and a single
sturdy occupant, the bed had developed a sag in the
middle so that it would have been easy to roll towards
each other. They were earlier to bed than usual and
sleep for the moment was beyond reach.

"The police never came near the gym all day,"
Polly said.

"That's good."

Silence came back but sleep was still only a dream.
She found that she was sliding gradually down the
slope. Soon, Polly could feel warmth. They were closer
together. She could feel a light pressure from his hip.

"Don't know what I'd have done if you hadn't been
here," Darryl said suddenly. "That Diana's a useless
animal."

"What *would* you have done?"

"Don't know. I'd probably have stayed in hospital
longer. I'd have had to. My leg would have been properly
bust up, but for you. And the gym would have got in a
real old mess with only Slasher to look after it. You've
been a proper godsend and no mistake. Seems like we
look after each other. Both for one and one for both,
sort of."

Polly felt contentment wash over her and with it came
sleepiness. Without thinking, she rolled onto her side into
her favourite sleeping position and her leg settled over
Darryl's thighs. Instantly she was wide awake. His good
leg was bare, muscled and hairy and she realised that he
would not have been able to get pyjama trousers over
his cast. She apologised quickly and began to roll back
but his hand gently held her knee where it was. "Don't
move," he said. "This is comforting. Sort of friendly."

"I'm not putting weight on your bad leg?"

"Not the least little bit."

The pressure of his cast was cold and hard but she decided to ignore it. Out of the next silence she said, "You're very shy, aren't you?"

The words had come out before she had time to think about them. She felt him brace himself and then slowly relax. "How did you know that?" he said. "I thought I'd learned to hide it."

"I sensed it. Little bits of body language. When we first met, it took some time before you were ready to meet my eye. You're relaxed with anyone you know but you tense up with strangers. Why is it? You've no need to be like that. You're not bad looking and God knows you can look after yourself."

"There's no why and wherefore when it comes to shyness." Darryl's voice was no more than a whisper in the dark. "Either you are or you aren't. And knowing somebody isn't what makes the difference, it's whether you're at ease with them. There are people that I could flatten with one hand behind my back but I stay away from them because they reduce me, inside, to jelly. I was at ease with you almost straight away." He fell silent for a few heartbeats. When he spoke again, he sounded surprised. "I've never talked about it before. In some ways, shyness isn't to do with what's happened before or what you are now, it's just whether you're the sort of person who's not confident about what he might do next to make a fool of himself."

Polly's sympathies were ready to overflow. "Is shyness the reason that you're what you are?"

"A wrestler? I suppose it's possible. When you're in the ring, it's all going your way. Even if you lose, you've put up a show. They say that actors are mostly shy."

"I didn't mean that."

"What then?"

"I meant," she said bravely, "is that why you became homosexual?"

"Who told you a thing like that?" he asked in a louder voice.

"You did."

"I'm damn sure I didn't. I only said that I didn't make love to girls."

"I don't understand." Polly considered withdrawing her leg, but she was too comfortable and the juxtaposition, as Darryl had said, was friendly.

"No, you wouldn't." She felt him sigh. "This is something else I've never talked about, maybe it's all part of the same thing, but it comes easier in the dark with a friend."

"Am I a friend?"

"The best. I'd better explain or it'll spoil things. Maybe it will anyway, but I hope not. I've the same desires as any other man. Maybe more. Big, big desires. Desperate longings. But that's all I've got. It never goes any further. There's something wrong with me. It's as if my body feels desire but doesn't know what it should be feeling next."

Polly began to re-appraise their relationship. She might have little practical experience beyond some petting with boys her own age but she was not wholly ignorant. She had had biology lessons at school. The *Kamasutra* and *The Perfumed Garden* had been almost required reading after lights out at boarding school. She moved her upper knee for a moment and confirmed that

147

he now had an enormous erection. So that was not what was missing. She was both concerned and curious. She forced herself to ask the unaskable. "Didn't you ever masturbate? Do you mind my asking?"

"It's all right. It's a relief to talk. No. I tried but nothing went any further. I even went to bed with a girl once. It went on and on – she seemed to like it that way, she said afterwards that I was the best ever. But nothing happened for me beyond the wanting. It was fine, almost beautiful, romantic, glamorous, I don't have the words, but it was sad. It was beautiful desire without a beautiful ending. It was unsatisfying and I felt awful afterwards."

Polly discovered that she could understand what he was telling her. Like Darryl, she knew that she wanted to go forward but had no idea what sensations should follow. Perhaps, when her time came, she would suffer the same hiatus between arousal and climax. Did you have to know what a sensation would have to feel like before you could experience it? But no. There had to be a first time for pain or hunger. Or love.

Her hand, without conscious volition on her part, had moved and was gently stroking his rigid shaft although he seemed to be unaware of the contact. She found that her breathing had quickened and her joints seemed to be shaking. "Do you know why?" she asked. "Have you asked a doctor?" Her hand seemed to know what it was doing.

"My God! I couldn't. I'm talking to you but I couldn't to anyone else in the world. Yes, I think I do know why. It's psychological. My dad died when I was young. My mum brought me up. I had four older sisters and no male relations to tell me what was what. I was simply brought up to believe that sex is wrong, that it simply doesn't and mustn't happen. That was drummed into me for all the most important years. Stupid, of course. If that was the way of it, the human race would have died out. And at school they carried on as though a good wank would be a passport to hell."

"Was that Mr Mahon?"

"No, he was all right. But the man they brought in to give biology lessons, I think he was queer. He described the science all right but avoided the act as if it was unmentionable. Something inside me believes that sexual pleasure's appallingly wicked."

They were quiet again. On the verge of sleep, Polly's mind was wandering. She was aware, without quite knowing how, that Darryl was wide awake. "What are we going to do about Diana?" she asked aloud. "If somebody drew up a list of the world's most self-centred women, she'd be sure of a place near the top."

"Can't you kick her out?" came Darryl's voice.

"You know we can't. Not unless we can find somewhere else for her to go."

"I think she has a mother up north somewhere, but she won't admit it as long as she's getting free board and lodging here. Polly, you can't take in everybody who has problems."

"But it's sort of my fault that she can't go back to her job or anywhere else."

"Sort of? If she was a pure little innocent she wouldn't be in this pickle. You didn't mean her any harm."

"I caused it all the same," Polly said unhappily.

"Not really. You created Daphne. You couldn't possibly have foreseen that Diana would be suspected – even if that's true. The woman's a pathological liar.

149

She's on a good thing," Darryl said irritably. "Fed and housed and no work to do. She doesn't even have to be somebody's mistress. She isn't going to move unless somebody sticks a pin in her. I can't afford to feed all of us for ever."

"You probably could," Polly said. "But it won't come to that."

"I'll see that it doesn't. If she's going to be around for a while. You'll have to find out if she's a properly trained masseuse and not just a sort of amateur tart with a cover story. If she can give proper massages to help strained muscles and ligaments, maybe we could take her to the gym and let her earn enough to pay some rent. We used to have a masseur come in on two evenings a week, but he went to South Africa and I never found anyone to take his place."

"Good idea," Polly said. "I'm sure she'd rather be earning her keep."

"I'm sure she wouldn't," Darryl said. "But we'll try it anyway."

During the silence that followed, Polly found that she was wholeheartedly sorry for Darryl. "About the other thing, you could be treated," she said.

"I'm not going to any bloody psychiatrists," Darryl said indignantly. "I can mess up my own mind without any outside help. No, I've resigned myself . . . to . . ." His voice trailed away. When he spoke again it was with real urgency. "Kiss me," he said. "Please, please, *please*." This at least was a request that Polly had met with before. She kissed him. It was like no kiss that she had even known before. He was the first to recover his tongue and break away. He pulled her roughly closer. "I think I know now what I should be feeling," he said hoarsely.

Polly might lack experience but she had no hangups about sex. She had once heard her mother tell an indignant vicar that, 'If God was going to be so shocked by a little sex, he shouldn't have made so much of it'. She thought furiously, counting from the date of her last period, and decided that she should be safe enough. "Don't move," she said. "We don't want any strain on your leg. I'm coming on top."

The size of him frightened her at first. But after a moment it felt right, the rightest thing in the world. She found that the gritty reality was not so gritty after all. Joy was taking over her whole body. Some minutes later, the household was roused by Darryl's roar of triumph. Polly managed to behave with more restraint.

Diana claimed to be a fully-trained masseuse. She seemed indignant even to be asked the question. The suggestion that she might leave her sanctuary and venture abroad brought all her fears to the surface, but when Polly pointed out that she would be surrounded by a phalanx of professional fighters she calmed down and expressed interest – but whether in the protection or in the fighters Polly was uncertain.

Polly was glad to get back to the garden and spent the morning pleasurably analysing her emotions. She also spared a thought for the implications beyond the vase. Should she call the attention of the police to the fact that Harry Hains had had a locker at the gym? When they came to realise it, would her silence seem suspicious? On the whole, she thought not. If they could overlook the possibility, so could she. And an increasing frequency of her contacts with

151

the police would surely lead to Daphne's unmasking in the end.

She thought that Darryl's leg was still paining him but he insisted on accompanying her to the gym, ostensibly to continue working out as much of his body as possible, but Polly suspected that his real motive might be that, having at last entered the land of silken pleasures, he wanted to relive the recurrent adventures of the night, if not in reality then in retrospect. He rarely let her move more than a few yards from his side and seemed to delight in any physical contact. To all of this, Polly had not the least objection. She had previously been looking on Darryl as a new but very good friend who could never be more; but after the night's tumultuous events her fondness had become . . . She hesitated at the thought. Among her contemporaries the word 'love' had only been used in jest. Now she wondered whether there might not be something in it.

Several of the regular clients were nursing minor muscular injuries. Most of the others had done so or could, in the nature of their various callings, expect to do so in the near future. The immediate consensus was that the departed masseur was sorely missed and that a female replacement might even be an improvement. It was arranged that Diana would attend on two or three days a week and one of the bodybuilders undertook to fetch her to and for in his elderly but immaculate Jaguar. It was clearly impossible for Polly to transport both Darryl and Diana on the scooter and Diana would certainly jib at public transport. When Polly went out to buy a crepe bandage for a weightlifter she used her own money to buy hair-dye and an overall.

The change of hair colour from artificial blonde to

near her natural black transformed and also, in Polly's opinion, improved Diana's appearance. Some careful makeup hid most of the bruising and even added strength to her face. On the appointed day, after some initial hesitation while she managed to rid herself of the conviction that hundreds of possible attackers were in the street and only waiting for her to come out and be recognised, she ventured across the few yards of pavement and into the Jaguar. She took over a corner of the big room, using for the purpose a trestle table borrowed from a nearby church hall, and although she still looked drawn – the result, Polly thought, of being deprived of her drug habit – she worked with a will. The remaining visible bruises were passed off as the aftermath of a road accident. She had three clients on that first afternoon and booked five appointments for the following Monday. She waited into the evening in case further business should arrive and then allowed the bodybuilder to convey her back to the house.

"That's okay then," Darryl said. "She'll be able to pay rent until I have to kick her out again."

"For my room?"

"I thought you were moving in with me."

"I am. But I may want to move out again if you're not good to me." Darryl looked thoughtful but was saved by the telephone from having to think of the right answer. Polly answered the call. Diana was on the line. "If you're home already," Polly said, "he drives too fast."

"There isn't a phone in your room," Diana said. "Had you forgotten? Listen, I stopped the car to call you from a pay-phone. As we pulled out, the car's lights shone across the front of the gym and I saw a man standing in the recess at the end of the building."

"Waiting for his girlfriend," said Polly. "Or maybe having a pee."

"Neither of those. He looked too furtive. I think he was lurking, waiting for me." The panic was back in her voice.

"If he was lurking," Polly said, "– and I've still to be convinced that you know a lurk when you see one – he was probably waiting for me to come out with the takings and go to the night-safe at the bank."

Diana wasn't listening. "I don't think I can risk coming out again," she said.

Polly felt that she had put up with more than enough nuisance from someone who had never been anything but a thorn in the flesh. "If you don't earn some money and pay your whack," she retorted, "I don't think we'll tolerate you much longer, freeloading and being a general pain in the bum. Pity can only be spread just so thin."

She hung up before Diana could retaliate. "Diana says there's somebody lurking outside," she told Darryl. "It's probably paranoia talking, but someone had better go and look around. Not you," she added quickly as he reached for his crutches. "The gym's still full of bruisers. I'll see if three or four of them will go and do a little street-cleaning."

But when Polly left the office for the big gym, she found that most of the evening's attendance had melted away. The last two clients were making for the door but these, a wrestler and a professional circus strongman, were ideally suited to her purpose and expressed themselves willing to do a favour for a woman and make sure that she was in no danger. Their tone was gallant if patronising – she half expected to be addressed as 'little lady' – but their manner was altogether different when they returned in very few seconds.

"There's a man out there all right," said the wrestler.

"I think he's dead," said the strongman. He sat down on a stool and put his head between his knees.

"It looks like somebody I used to see in here," said the wrestler.

"It's Harry Hains," said the strongman in a muffled voice. "You'd better call the police. And an ambulance, in case he's still alive."

Darryl was getting up but again Polly restrained him. "Stay in here," she said. "If we go out there, we'll be witnesses and they'll keep us forever." The Emergency Services answered the call and she passed the two messages. "How did he die?" she asked.

"Messily," said the wrestler. He bolted for the toilet.

Nine

D arryl reached for his crutches, intending to make his clumsy way outside and take a look for himself, but Polly called him back. She pointed out in an urgent whisper that they might thereby become witnesses to something-or-other with all the attendant nuisance (and, she added silently, publicity and police attention, of which she had already had more than she welcomed). In the faint hope of remaining uninvolved, Darryl stayed in the office and Polly set about the evening's cleaning, but neither's mind was wholly on the tasks and it took half a day, much later, to sort out the tangle that Darryl had made of the VAT figures. The wrestler (who was professionally known as Springheel Jack because of his talent for standing drop-kicks) stood at the gym door, where he had the benefit of fresh air to settle his very much upset stomach, and gave a running commentary on events.

The ambulance arrived first. It seemed, from their reluctance to remove the patient, that the paramedics did not detect any life-signs. A police surgeon dead-heated with the first police car and must have agreed with them. Activity in the yard thereafter developed rapidly as the routine of investigation began. Vehicles could be heard arriving. Blue lights flashed and died. Blinks of

157

white light glimpsed under the door and through the rooflights indicated that a photographer was at work.

A plain-clothes officer soon came in search of the finders of the body. He identified himself as Detective Inspector Something – Polly only half-caught the name but thought that it sounded like Colander. The DI won Polly's immediate approval. He was informally dressed for evening duty, in a polo-neck and tweed jacket, but his brogues were glossy and his trousers were well pressed. Polly decided to hold him up as an example for Darryl.

Springheel Jack and the strongman were led out to a Range Rover and transferred to the incident room. The connection with Patrick Mahon's death must have been established immediately because this, they learned later, was the incident room already in use nearby. Somebody else must have been conducting the interviews because the Detective Inspector returned within a few minutes. He was accompanied by a woman in a severe business suit whom he identified as a WPC.

The office was too small for more than two people to sit at a time. The big gym had benches against the walls and they settled in a corner. Polly made sure that Darryl's leg was comfortable. "You can see that Mr Davidson is injured," she said. "He didn't see or hear anything. Can't he go home? I could call him a taxi."

"This shouldn't take long," the DI said. "I'm sure that he can endure for another minute or two. I understand that there was a phonecall."

Polly silently damned whichever of the two gladiators had brought that up. "I took it," she said.

"Your name?"

Polly gave the name on her mother's driving licence

and the address of Darryl's house. Without going beyond the immediate facts, she explained Diana's presence as a masseuse and recounted that part of the phonecall concerned with the lurking man. If the police interviewed Diana, as they surely must, it would be for Diana herself to decide how much to reveal of her fears and the reason behind them.

The DI looked at Darryl. "You didn't hear the phonecall?"

"No."

"Nor see the body?"

"No."

"I understand that the dead man has been identified as Henry Hains and that Hains was a frequent attender here."

"I didn't see the body," Darryl pointed out.

"Harry Hains came regularly until a week ago," Polly said. "He told us that he was getting ready for a circus job in Russia which he later told me didn't come off."

The DI switched his suddenly sharpened attention back to her and then looked at the WPC. "I think we can let Mr Davidson go for the moment," he said. "I suggest that you drive him home and come back."

The WPC looked surprised. Polly thought that it could not be usual for a DI to ask to be left alone with a woman witness. But evidently one or both of them were judged to be trustworthy, because the WPC went to the door. Darryl looked questioningly at Polly and then followed.

When the big door had closed, the DI said, "I don't want to keep you longer than I have to. We'll get on a lot quicker if we come out into the open. You're Daphne, aren't you?"

159

For the first few seconds, Polly was confused. So much had happened in such quick succession that her sobriquet had, for the moment, gone out of her mind. Then she dithered. She considered a flat denial. But a denial would almost certainly be disbelieved, whereas it would be a relief to talk, and she came from a background in which the police were considered to be helpful if sometimes aggravating public servants until proved otherwise. Also, the Detective Inspector was well spoken and had what she thought of as an honest and open face. She sighed. "How did you find out?" she asked.

The Detective Inspector smiled. His smile was friendly, showing straight, white teeth, and Polly thought that she made the right decision. At least he was not going to be angry at her for her oblique approach. "We've been collecting the voice-prints of every woman known to have any connection with anyone involved in the case and comparing them with those from the two phonecalls."

"I only spoke half a dozen words before the sergeant switched off the tape recorder," Polly said.

"Half a dozen words are enough. It took until today to get the results." He shook his head in disgust. "If you try to hurry the lab they just move your work to the back of the queue. But I'd have known you anyway. I must have listened to the tapes of your two calls at least twenty times. You've lived in several different places and gone to different schools, haven't you?"

"All over the place," Polly admitted.

He nodded, pleased with his own powers of reasoning. "Your voice has no consistent accent but you have a distinctive rhythm and pitch. We'd have got onto you sooner if you hadn't pretended to be a former pupil of Mr Mahon – which you weren't, I think?"

"No," Polly admitted.

"That was ingenious. Are you going to come clean now?"

Polly had been asking herself the same question. "Are you in charge of the investigation?" she asked abruptly.

"This one or the death of Patrick Mahon? But no." He checked himself. "If we go on asking each other questions we'll get nowhere. For the moment, I'm in charge here but detective inspectors don't usually head murder inquiries. But never mind that. You've been very elusive. If you think that you have any reason to be afraid of the police, I can assure you that I am interested only in these two deaths. Unless, of course, you've killed somebody else . . . ?"

Polly decided that he was pulling her leg. "No, of course not," she said.

"I'm relieved. You've been helpful and we're grateful but I think you may have some more to tell us. I assume that you were hiding behind an alias out of fear – not of the police but of the – somebody else." Polly nodded. "I could make a reasoned guess as to who," said the DI.

"If I should think of something else to tell you—" Polly began.

The DI understood immediately. "You may have wasted some police time by holding back, but I promise you that we'll overlook it if you come clean now. You have my word. How about it?"

Polly looked up into the cobwebbed void of the roof while she thought about it. That was all very well, she decided, as far as it went, but it did not go very far. "Can

161

you keep my identity confidential or will I have to run away and hide? Colander, as a name, doesn't inspire a lot of confidence."

The smile came back and turned into a chuckle. "My name's Calendar not Colander, and I don't leak like one." He sobered. "I can understand your caution and I admit it's not unknown for things to leak out from the police, but it is unusual for it to happen in this force. I don't think that it would happen in this case but you never know. You've had a lot of publicity both as Daphne and – am I right? – as the young lady who leapt into the ring in defence of Mr Davidson and almost flattened Frankie Delrose. All I can say is this: we're aware of the danger and so we never make the identities of informants known beyond the absolutely essential. Your voice, for instance, went to the lab marked only with a serial number. Inevitably, some people will make the connection. It is just possible that some hungry young copper might sell the story to the media, either for cash or in the hope of favours in return to advance his career. If he does, he'll be found and prosecuted, and that fact is well known."

"There you are, then."

"However," said the Detective Inspector firmly, "as I said, I don't think that it will happen. And it's quite customary for an officer to keep his sources of information secret – up to a certain point. That point may be reached when a case is being prepared for court, if the informant's evidence is necessary. But, by that time, you could expect that anybody who was a threat would be locked up."

"Or out on bail," Polly said.

"Not if there's strong case and the police oppose

bail on the grounds that witnesses might be threatened."

"You might have Ronald Dent inside by then, but he had others to do his work for him."

"He has a couple of cronies," Detective Inspector Calendar admitted. "But he never had what you could call a regular gang. The man you described in your second phonecall is securely in jail and likely to remain there, because fibres were found on him from Mr Mahon's carpet and when arrested he began uttering threats. Bail will not be an option."

"Harry Hains got bail," Polly pointed out.

"He was no danger to witnesses and we hoped that he might lead us to the others or to the vase. I'm afraid that he was too slippery for that. Dent's other two regular associates don't seem to be quite so keen to follow him anymore. In fact, they're believed to be in London and keeping their heads well down." He paused and looked at her with no trace of his earlier smile. "We couldn't spare the men to give you round-the-clock protection. But as long you don't do anything to invite attention from Mr Dent, I honestly don't think that it would be called for. We could have the patrol cars take a look here and at your home whenever they go past, but—"

"But that would give me away to the rest of the fuzz," Polly broke in. "Do you mind being called fuzz?"

"I've been called very much worse."

Polly capitulated. "All right, I'll tell you what I know. But I'll think about it again when the time comes for a court case and, in the meantime, if I think that my identity has been leaked to anyone – anyone at all – you suddenly won't see me around anymore. Clear?"

The smile was back. "Perfectly. But check with

me before doing a runner. You could be mistaken."

"I suppose so." Once she had begun to talk, Polly found that every last detail came out or was coaxed out of her – with one monumental exception. Even Diana's sufferings were laid bare. "I suppose you'll have to talk to her?" Polly said.

"Inevitably."

A day or two earlier, Polly would have been only too delighted if the police had carried Diana off and subjected her to all the rigours the law allowed and more but, now that she had begun to put herself back together, Polly found that she had developed a protective attitude towards Diana. "Well, go easy on her," she said. "Please. She's scared and she's having to go without her – her bad habit. Could you wait until Thursday? I think it would panic her less if you interviewed her when she comes back here. If you see her at home, she'll begin to feel that nowhere's safe."

The Detective Inspector held Polly's eye for some seconds. His eyes, she noticed, were dark blue. "Her evidence isn't urgent yet and we have plenty to get on with. I can do that. I may even have developed more questions to ask her by then. You've certainly told us nearly as much we can expect from her. But can I trust her not to run off?"

"You can trust me," Polly said. "If I think that she's going to panic and run for it, I'll phone you. Can I tell her that you won't come down on her for possession of prohibited substances, or whatever the wording is?"

"I'm not looking for drugs at the moment. If she hasn't been selling them to anyone else, I'll forget them. Go on with your tale."

When Polly came to a halt at last, DI Calendar said, "You'll make a good witness. You've laid it out logically. Is this how you see it? Ronald Dent agreed with this American dealer to steal a very valuable Chinese vase. He sent Henry Hains and the other man – whose name, by the way, is Hermitage – to do the job. By mistake, in the process, they killed Patrick Mahon. Your friend's boyfriend, Hugo Tyrone, was to have taken it out of the country on one of his trips as an airline steward. But the value of the stolen object is very large, quite large enough to tempt Tyrone to double-cross Dent. The phone number that you found in the purse suggests that Tyrone was planning to do his own deal with a different collector and fade away. Hains may have been planning the same thing and been killed for it. Yes?"

"That's how I was looking at it," Polly admitted.

"It's a tenable theory, but no more than that. If it's right, then there's a high probability that Hains was the intruder on the roof. He didn't manage to break in that way. So he was hanging around outside here – lurking, in your friend's words – in the hope of inducing you to let him in after the clients had all gone, or breaking in through the door. Right?"

"Right," Polly said, as cheerfully as she could manage. "Of course," she added, "the two of them may have been in partnership. Either way, the vase may be out of the country by now." She could guess what was coming but there was nothing that she could do about it. The vase was not in Harry Hains's locker.

She was right. "You have lockers here?"

"Yes."

"Hains had one?"

"I expect so. Most of the regulars rent a locker." She

165

led the way to the office and made a show of finding
Darryl's list. "Yes. The list only shows who rent lockers.
I don't know which one Harry Hains used."

"Then we'd better take a look for it." DI Calendar got
to his feet as the plain clothes WPC knocked on the door
and walked in. "Show me. You have a master-key?"

Too little knowledge might arouse suspicions as
readily as too much. "I've seen him go to this end
of the row," she said.

"Then we'll start here."

The second locker had been Harry Hains's. Polly
claimed to recognise his circus costumes. The Detective
Inspector nodded to the WPC, who drew on a pair of
paper gloves and began to feel among the garments.
"There's no vase in here," she said immediately.

"Interesting," Calendar said. "Why would he be so
keen to gain access, unless . . ." The WPC turned round
with a flat box in her hands. The box had once held
cigars. The DI nodded and she opened it, revealing a
hoard of paper money. "This could explain a certain
determination," Calendar said. "But why not call in for
it openly?"

"That I can't tell you," Polly said. "But I gave you
Hains's name only about a day after the crime and it
was on the News soon afterwards. There were some
former pupils of Mr Mahon among the members and
he seems to have been surprisingly popular, considering
that he was a headmaster. They're mostly very mild
men outside of the ring, but they were beginning to
breathe fire and slaughter. Any one of them could
have pulled Harry Hains's head off and stuffed it
down his throat, and they'd have done it, too. And
I suppose he felt extra vulnerable, with his savings in

the locker. Can I finish cleaning and go now? It's past my bedtime."

"There'll be no more cleaning tonight. There will have to be a thorough search. The vase could be hidden somewhere else in here. Or in another locker."

Polly had had enough for one day. She led the two officers back to the office and compared the register of locker users with the keys in Darryl's locked drawer. "There aren't any lockers unaccounted for," Polly said. "I don't think that you should go through all the lockers unless Mr Davidson or I are present. Search all you want for the old vase, but I'll take the master-key home with me and open up the lockers for you in the morning. Lock up and turn the lights out when you finish will you?"

"*If* we finish. All right, I'll accept your terms," Calendar said. "I don't hold much hope of the other lockers anyway. But, before you leave, would you two ladies count this money for me and write down the agreed total?"

The killing of Harry Hains proved to be another seven day wonder. The locals discussed it, the local media were full of it but Polly's presence near the scene was barely mentioned. As a minor relief, there was still no connection made between her and the young lady who had been seen on television to fell a wrestler in the ring.

Polly managed to keep pace with the household chores but had little time to spare for gardening. She kept watch while the lockers were searched and the searchers went on to probe the athletic equipment and, later, the long-forgotten, dusty, spider-infested interstices of the building. This took several days, during which the gym was allowed to reopen but Polly, aided by any clients who she managed to press into service, was continually struggling to restore order and to clear out the dust of ages which had been disturbed by the search. Two of the searchers enrolled for judo classes and another made a booking for a massage. Polly was satisfied that they were in pursuit of health and fitness rather than information.

On the second day of the search, while Darryl was resting his leg at home, the sergeant in charge – a stern and fussy, older, plain-clothes man whom Polly decided had been passed over for promotion and resented the fact – requested her company in a far corner of the gym beside the showers. An insulated pipe, one of many, ran along the wall. He pointed to several places where the two halves of the polystyrene insulation were held together with sticky tape.

"So what's the problem?" Polly asked him. "Have we offended against the building regulations?"

The sergeant was not amused. "See here," he said, pointing. Elsewhere, the insulation was fastened with ties that looked to Polly like nylon. "Some of these are missing," he said.

"So?"

"Ties like these were used to tie up Patrick Mahon."

"Really?" Polly looked more closely. "I've used ties like these to fasten tree-guards in the garden. They keep rabbits from chewing the bark of young trees."

The sergeant was not interest in gardening reminiscences. "How long have these been missing?"

'I've no idea," Polly admitted. 'I'll ask Mr Davidson, if you like. Does it really matter? Once the plain end's pushed through the slot at the other end, you can't pull it back again."

"You can if you push the little tab down with a small screwdriver," said the sergeant. "Otherwise, they're very effective. Some countries use them instead of handcuffs."

Polly looked again. "That tape's been in place for ages," she said. "It's filthy. And why would anyone want to pinch a few nylon ties from here when you can buy a big bag of them from a builder's merchant for pennies? But I'll ask Mr Davidson."

She phoned Darryl from the office. He confirmed that the insulation had already been taped in several places when he took over the building.

To Polly's surprise Diana, once Polly had passed on a message from DI Calendar to the effect that Hugo had failed to rejoin his plane in New York for a return journey and had not come back to Britain by any other route, calmed down and seemed quite willing to meet the Inspector for questioning.

Ronald Dent remained at large. In a private interview, DI Calendar explained to an increasingly nervous Polly that there was still no evidence linking Dent with any of the various offences except Polly's testimony that he had been seen studying a photograph of the missing vase in the company of the two suspects – evidence which would be unlikely to stand up on its own. "After all," Calendar said, "any competent lawyer could argue that he had been admiring the vase and had not the least idea in the world that the two naughty boys intended to go after it." The word, which reached Polly by way of some of the less reputable clients at the gym, was that Dent

169

was enjoying, on the surface at least, his usual round of booze and dolly-birds but that he was also asking a lot of people a lot of questions, with offers of money or threats of violence as might be appropriate. He wanted to know the whereabouts of Hugo Tyrone and whether any others of his own past or present associates had either headed for the hills or assumed a sudden air of prosperity, but most of all he wanted to know what evidence the police had against himself and where they had obtained it. Polly hoped that he would never know.

By the Thursday, the fuss was already dying down. Polly's belief was that the police were only interested in the death of the cat-burglar (who appeared also to be guilty of manslaughter) insofar as it might enable them to take Ronald Dent out of circulation. A much higher priority was put on the recovery of the Chinese vase, but more in the hope of preventing any dishonest person from re-importing its value in the form of drugs than from any nobler motive. Its failure to arrive at its intended place in the museum was not regarded as a national disaster except by the museum authorities. The great rarity of fourteenth century Chinese porcelain was only of public interest as reflected in its cash value.

Detective Inspector Calendar came to the gym for his appointment with Diana. At the last moment, Diana's courage seemed about to fail her and she asked if Polly could be present. The gym was not yet open so they settled in the same corner as before. WPC Nicholls was there to take notes again and, Polly assumed, to act as chaperone.

The Detective Inspector began by recording the names of those present. Darryl's address was public knowledge and it was becoming widely known that Polly resided in the same house. Her sharing of his bed was suspected by most of the clients at the gym, thanks to the rosy glow that seemed to surround them whenever they were within sight of one another. Diana's return to her former address was known at least to the strongman who was acting as her chauffeur and so could hardly be considered a well-kept secret. Nevertheless, advertising any of those facts through the police grapevine could do no good and might just prove to be the last breath of air on the wrong side of the scales. Polly had insisted that DI Calendar keep addresses off the record.

"First, the good news," Calendar began. "At least, I think it's good news and you'll probably agree. Hugo Tyrone – whose real name, by the way, is John Herd – is in custody in New York and likely to remain there. As you know, he failed to rejoin the plane after an overnight stop. At our request, the NYPD found bank accounts in both his names, watched them and picked him up. He turned out to be in possession of hard drugs. It seems that he had earlier been acting as a courier in a fairly minor way. It also seems that he had taken fright at the news of Patrick Mahon's death and decided to sever his ties with this country and to work instead for his American contacts.

"Now, I understand, Miss Stubbs, that you were assaulted and that, out of fear, you made no report to the police. Is that correct?"

Diana, her voice barely rising above a whisper, said that it was.

"And your assailant was – I suggest that we continue to refer to him as Hugo Tyrone. It's the name we know him by and I'm sure that he'd prefer it. Well?"

Diana produced a tremulous smile and nodded.

"That's a yes. The burning question, then, is why? Why did he beat you up and why has he done a bolt? And are the two things connected?"

"He knew that I wouldn't make a complaint," Diana said.

"I don't suggest that he fled the country for fear of the consequences of his attack on you," Calendar said patiently. "What I'm suggesting is that both actions were the result of something that you knew?"

Diana shook her dark head. Polly noticed that her hair was now growing out brown at the roots. "Well, I can't think what."

"Or were thought to know?"

"I knew that he was an evil bastard," Diana said. "He made no secret of it, away from his job. He was even proud of it. He boasted about it. But he said that I was special and that he would always be loving and tender with me." She drew in a tremulous breath. "He kept his word until that last day. And he could turn on some real charm, when he wanted." Her voice quivered but she went bravely on. "He used to give me coke to sniff. It gave me an enormous high. I thought he was being generous and kind and helping me to cope with life, but I suppose he just wanted to have me hooked."

"And are you?" Polly asked quickly.

"Hooked?" They waited while Diana gave it her consideration. Evidently, she had never bothered to look inside herself. "I don't think so," she said at last. "Not really. It was more a social sort of habit, like getting pissed now and again. I knew that he was bringing the stuff in but I thought it was just for me and a few friends. After he beat me up, I'd've given the earth for a fix just to kill all the pain, but coming off it wasn't really what hurt. Now, after this time . . . I know that a fix would make me feel good but I'm not desperate for it anymore. I won't go back now. Honestly." Not until the next unscrupulous bastard comes along, Polly thought. She could see that the Detective Inspector was similarly unconvinced, but he had weightier matters to pursue.

"Did he and Ronald Dent know each other?"

"They knew each other. But they never seemed to want to be seen together."

"Tell me what was said when he beat you up."

"Not much." Diana flinched at the memory. "It was what they call actions speaking louder than words. He just came home in a hell of a temper and rained on me with his fists. When I fell down he – he kicked me. He was calling me names, but mostly he called me Daphne."

"You knew what he meant?"

"Of course. It was all over the TV. And the radio."

"Why would he think you were Daphne?"

"I don't know. I didn't know anything about his . . . other business. And I didn't want to know, he knew that. We both wanted it that way."

"But could he have thought that you knew something?"

"He might have." There was a long pause while Diana thought back. "There was only the one time," she said at last. "I was sitting by the bedroom window. I was sewing. There was an open seam in my shirt and I wasn't buying a new one," she added defensively, as though the sign of domestication might somehow have been against her feminist principles. "I heard Hugo come in. He had somebody with him. I recognised Ronnie Dent's voice

– the door was slightly open and you can hardly mistake it – and I think there was another man."

"You didn't join the party?"

"I knew I'd be sent to pour drinks or make coffee and I wanted to finish what I was doing."

"But you heard what was said?" Calendar asked eagerly.

"Sort of. I heard but I wasn't paying any attention. Well, it was nothing to do with me. But when they'd gone, Hugo came into the bedroom for something and found me there and he hit the ceiling and wanted to know why I hadn't spoken up and whether I'd been listening and what I'd heard. I told him that I hadn't heard a damn thing but he didn't believe me. He kept on and on saying that I mustn't tell a soul or I'd get myself into trouble as well as him. That's probably why he thought that I was Daphne," she said brightly. "And he hummed and hawed and then said that we'd better not let Dent know that I'd heard anything and I told him again that I *hadn't* heard anything but he still didn't seem to believe me."

The DI had had experience with rambling witnesses. "You told us that you had 'sort of' heard something."

"Well, yes. Sort of. But nothing I could swear to in court."

Polly had decided to contribute moral support and nothing else, but Detective Inspector Calendar seemed to be making heavy weather. "You must have got a general idea of what they were talking about," she suggested.

Diana had come to accept Polly as a sort of authority figure. "Well, yes," she said. "Sort of. It was about a thing."

The DI, who had brightened, now looked pained. "What thing?"

"I don't know. A thing. Wing or ping or ding, I don't remember."

"Could it have been Ming?" Calendar asked.

Diana shrugged, managing to make her breasts bob with the movement. "Same difference," she said coyly. "It was a thing that had to go somewhere. I think Hugo was supposed to take it, but I could have got that wrong. The bit I did hear was that they were arguing about who was to look after it between when they got it and when it went away again. That's when I think something was said about Hugo making his next flight to somewhere. I remember New York was mentioned, because I've never been there."

DI Calendar seemed to have lost heart. He questioned Diana for another ten minutes without stimulating her memory any further and then gave up and left. Polly opened the gym for business.

Darryl would be expecting her to return for him, but first Polly decided to satisfy her own curiosity. She sought out one of the more susceptible of the searchers (who were still finding more and more remote corners of the building to pry into) and by a mixture of coaxing and flattery persuaded him to divulge details of Harry Hains's death which had so far not been made public. Hains had been killed, rather gruesomely, by a cheap clasp-knife which had been left at the scene. There had been no fingerprints. His killer would certainly have got blood on his clothes. Against that, some clothing had been doused with petrol and burned on a vacant site half a mile away. From the fragments and the quantity of ash remaining, it had been a boiler suit of a large size.

175

"Large enough to go over his other clothes," she said to Darryl that evening. "And the clasp-knife had been sharpened until you could have shaved with it, I was told. That sounds as if Dent or what's-his-name – Hermitage – meant all along to kill Harry Hains."

"Maybe," Darryl said. "Or at least that he was prepared to kill him if all other arguments failed. I mean, he wouldn't set out to kill him. Not until after he got the pot back. You know what I think? I think the vase may have been hidden somewhere just outside the gym. From what I hear, Ronnie Dent's more interested in who shopped him than where the pot's got to. I think he's already got it back."

Polly wanted to avoid that subject. "And you know what I think?" she said quickly. "I think it's about our bedtime."

"I like your thought better than mine," Darryl said.

Ten

The next week saw a period of hectic activity. The police were busy, asking many questions but apparently not receiving many satisfactory answers. Reporters were also busy and, failing real news, a great deal of unsupported speculation found its way into print. And the gym was busy. Darryl, in search of an alternative source of income while waiting for his leg to heal, had begun coaching aspiring wrestlers and as the word went round this proved a surprisingly popular service. Southhill Comprehensive School, Patrick Mahon's former charge, sent several boys, as did a local youth club. There was even word of a self-defence class for girls. Darryl's clumsy plaster cast had been replaced by a more streamlined version in mouldable plastic, but he still needed his crutches. Slasher was recruited to give any physical demonstrations. Diana stopped jumping at shadows and recovered confidence although, for quite different reasons, she still insisted on being chauffeured to and fro by the strongman.

Thursday came round again. And events took a twist that, for the moment, put murder and mayhem and even Ming vases out of Polly's mind. Diana and the clients had left and Polly, already showered after her own workout, was sweeping the barn-like room when Darryl took a

177

phonecall in the office. He humped himself out on his crutches. "That was Mr Franklyn, from the casino," he said. "He wants us to pay him a call as soon as we're finished here."

"I'm tired," Polly said. "It's you he wants to see. Surely I'm not needed?"

"He seemed to want you in particular."

"What's it about?"

"No idea." Darryl paused, evidently weighing up the balance of free drinks against any delay to the resumption of his lovelife. "We'd better go," he said at last. "It doesn't do to fall out with people."

"I suppose so," Polly said without enthusiasm. "I'll drop you at the door of the casino and join you in ten minutes or so after I've made myself sort of respectable. Okay?"

"Okay."

When Polly entered the basement bar only slightly behind her promised time, most of the drinkers had already departed, leaving only smoke and stale air, spilled drinks and ashtrays filled with stubs. Darryl was back at their usual corner table with a pint in front of him. Polly had dragooned him into buying a jacket of rather better fit and had herself altered his much abused trousers, and she thought that he was looking very presentable. He was talking, rather solemnly, with the Franklyns.

Polly, who had never before seen them together, was stuck by the contrast between the couple. Mrs Franklyn had a style and air of confidence which her husband, though dressed for the job and definitely in command, seemed to lack. Polly, who was fast becoming wise beyond her years, decided that Mrs Franklyn had married beneath her and dragged her husband up the ladder of success. She was in no doubt of the affection between them. Her own love for Darryl had rendered her sensitive to little nuances of voice and look and touch.

When Polly was seated with a drink in her hand, Darryl said, "She'd better hear this for herself. I'm not her keeper."

Polly took a sip from her spritzer. "Hear what?" she asked.

The Franklyns glanced at each other and by some invisible signals Mr Franklyn was elected to speak. "It's this way," he said. "Above here, we have catering and rooms for cardgames, mostly private parties. At the back, there's a big room that started life as a church hall. The church was pulled down years ago. Darryl's seen the room. That's where the public come and play roulette, blackjack, you name it. There are gaming machines. It's profitable, but the whole place costs a mint to run in salaries and security and you-name-it, so we have to keep the revenue coming. That means attracting people in for a first visit and then making sure they want to come back.

"Most nights, we have a pianist playing softly, you can just about hear him. Nothing loud enough to distract people just when they want to concentrate. Mozart and all that. Creates the right atmosphere, Fiona says."

"You haven't had any complaints, have you?" Mrs Franklyn said. It was not a question.

"No," Mr Franklyn admitted. 'Anyway, the weekends look after themselves, more or less. Friday nights, when men are unwinding and feeling rich, we want to draw them in. Then, win or lose, they may come back over the weekend to recoup their losses or build on their winnings. So we have a refreshment break and a small cabaret. The pianist gets to cut loose for a minute or two and then there's some other entertainer. Sometimes it's been a singer. Can you dance?"

Polly was a little taken aback by the change of subject, but it seemed to be an easy question to answer. "I've had dance lessons," she said. "I grew too tall for ballet but my mother insisted that I go on. She said that it taught me to carry myself well and not slouch around like the others."

"Thought so," said Mr Franklyn. "You move well."

Polly thanked him. "I'm okay at disco," she said. "I'm not so hot in the ballroom and I can't do tap. What else do you want to know? And why?"

"How would you like to dance on stage?"

Immediately, Polly's interest was caught. She had always had a secret hankering for showbusiness. "Tell me about it," she said.

"That's right," Darryl said. "Tell her about it."

The Franklyns exchanged a glance and Mrs Franklyn took over. "The highlight that brings them in has always been an exotic dancer."

"Nothing vulgar," Mr Franklyn said quickly. "Always in the best of taste, as somebody used to say on the telly."

"Of course," said his wife. "Definitely."

"Of course. But the lady who did the act for us – and she is a lady, make no mistake about that – she got married this week and her husband doesn't want her to do it no more."

"*Any* more," his wife whispered.

"Any more. Well, I suppose it's understandable. And

180

there are others but they're not the same class act. And they're managed by a Greek bastard who I can't stand at any price." Mr Franklyn scowled and raised his several chins. "He's no better than a pimp and I've told him so to his face. So he won't play ball."

"Not that we could put up with the acts he handles anyway," said Mrs Franklyn. "Coarse. They'd lower the tone and distract people from the gambling. What's worse, they'd alienate the women and the wives and girlfriends would immediately decide that it was time to go home."

Polly felt a huge giggle building up in her. "Are you by any chance talking about a stripper?" she asked.

"Only the best," Mrs Franklyn said hurriedly. "Something ladylike. The acts that that Greek handles wouldn't suit our clientele at all. Sluts dragging off what are obviously fancy costumes while they do obscene dances and make no secret of despising their customers. That's not what men really want, not around here anyway."

She was opening another window into a strange, new world and Polly, always ready to learn about the ways of people, was intrigued. "What *do* men want?" she asked.

"They're all different," Mrs Franklyn said with a shrug.

She was going to go on but her husband broke in. "What they *don't* want," he said, "is a lot of naked female flesh. That's what they're usually shown. But what do you think a man's most afraid of?" He waited, but Polly had no answer for him. "Castration, that's what. It's his most deep-seated instinct," he said with feeling. "And to many of them, maybe most of them, a woman's body can seem like his own mirror image, castrated."

181

Darryl was nodding in spite of himself. Polly made a great effort to imagine herself like a man. "I think I can understand that," she said. "Sort of."

"Be that as it may," said Mrs Franklyn haughtily, "rather than have a lot of overblown female flesh thrust at them, most men would rather see a pretty girl in pretty undies, undressing modestly. That's delicate, feminine and captivating. It signals the letting down of a barrier, not a vulgar invitation."

Mr Franklyn waved to the barmaid for repeats. "And also," he said, "it's making a show of what a woman wears that a man doesn't. It's a badge of femininity. The differences, but the unthreatening differences. Almost a uniform that says, 'Don't be afraid of me, I'm a girl, nothing to do with your fears.' See what I mean?" He was looking at Polly.

"I think so," she said. "But why are you telling me all this?"

"They can't get anyone else by tomorrow night," Darryl said. "They wonder if you'd take it on."

"Me? You want me to do a strip?" Polly wondered whether to laugh, storm out indignantly or hear more.

"Why not?" asked Mrs Franklyn. "You've got a lovely figure and we both thought that you moved like a dancer. You'd be a sensation. I could rehearse you."

Mr Franklyn received and distributed fresh drinks. "Fiona has lots of what you'd need," he said. "She likes to have pretty things. And you're much of a size."

"We could work up a really nice act," said his wife. "Dignified and not too revealing. You needn't feel sullied at all." She looked at Polly appraisingly. "You're not shocked, are you?"

"No," Polly said. "I'm not shocked." Although her

experience of sex was limited and recent, she had not
found it shocking but natural and full of delight. And
she was proud of her body. "But can't you get somebody
else? One of the gamblers? Let somebody pay off her
debts that way?"

"God! Have you seen them?" Mr Franklyn asked. "I'd
pay most of them to keep their clothes *on*. There'd be
a fee." He mentioned a figure which to Polly seemed
enormous. "That's much more than we'd usually pay, of
course, but the circumstances are special. We don't want
our customers being disappointed and developing the
habit of going somewhere else. That's the first principle
of bad management."

"What do you think?" Polly asked Darryl.

"I'm not going to tell you what to do," he said. "You're
your own girl."

"I'm always telling you what to do."

"So you are. But that doesn't mean that I have to be
a bossy-boots too."

Polly let that go by. "But would you *mind?*" she
asked.

Mrs Franklyn chose the perfect psychological moment.
"You'd have all the men envying you," she told
Darryl.

Darryl thought it over for a few seconds and said,
"No, I wouldn't mind. As long as I was there to see
that nothing else went on. After all, who would I be to
object? I show off my muscles and I know that some
girls come to see them. Men come to see the wrestling
but women come to see the muscles."

Polly would have preferred time to think it over, but
the Franklyns seemed to be waiting for an answer. "I
never did mind going topless," she said. "I've done that

often enough on the beach when Mum and I went abroad. After all, men have nipples too. But—"

"You could keep a thong," Mrs Franklyn said. "Or more. I've got an idea for an act. We could make it funny, but very prim. I've always felt that there was room for a comedy stripper. If I was younger, I'd do it myself."

That was a convincing argument. Polly had always fancied herself as a comedienne. It had been her favourite fantasy since she first discovered that an amusing answer would turn away wrath. "All right," she said. "I'll do it."

Polly woke in the morning with a sense of great events pending. When her promise of the previous evening came back to her, she felt hollow. She had embarked on her new existence with all the confidence of youth and of one who had had to cope with everything that an unsettled life could throw at her. She had made up her mind that she would pick up every gauntlet and meet every challenge face to face.

That was well and good, in theory. But had she perhaps bitten off more than she was prepared to chew? Was she in danger of stepping over even her mother's lax boundaries? Her only mental image of a stripper was derived from films seen on television, in which blowsy ladies narrowly evaded clutching hands while they writhed and swayed. Too late to back out of it now. Or was it? Surely nobody could force her to go through with a contract entered into so informally and when she had been, she was now sure, quite under the influence of several spritzers.

She ferried Darryl to the gym and left him there. He

would come to join her by taxi and it was a measure of his satisfaction with life in general that he intended to pay for it out of his own pocket. But Polly rode the scooter home, parked it in the hall and walked down the street to the casino.

Mrs Franklyn was awaiting her. That lady had been certain that the afternoon and early evening would allow time enough for costume fittings and rehearsal. Polly was beginning to feel that a lifetime would not be long enough, but she followed docilely while she was led through and shown a dauntingly huge but lavishly decorated room with space for what looked like thousands of gamblers around the tables occupying the centre of the room. Other tables round the walls, Mrs Franklyn explained, were for those who had retired from the fray to lick their wounds or refresh themselves with food or drink. From there, they climbed a private stair to the Franklyns' apartment on the topmost floor. Mr and Mrs Franklyn occupied separate bedrooms and Polly was led into a very feminine room, all fuss and frills. The waterbed took the form of a slender four-poster with looped-back muslin curtains and a mirror in the ceiling. The Franklyns' marriage, it seemed, was still alive and Mrs Franklyn had every intention of keeping it so. Polly looked and learned.

Away from the public eye, Mrs Franklyn showed a less formal side. Almost, she could be seen to let down her hair. "Call me Fiona," she said. "Or Fifi if you like. That's what hubby calls me when we're alone. We'll get along better, Ducky, if we cut out the formality. Now here," and she began pulling out drawers, "we have the makings of your act. He always likes me to have the best in lingerie."

185

Polly had a clear recollection of Mr Franklyn insisting that it was his wife whose taste ran to the luxurious in underwear, but she contented herself with admiring what seemed to be a mountain of silks and laces. This was no sensible body-covering from M & S, nor were the delicate fabrics intended for the pleasure of the wearer. These goods were meant to be seen and experienced.

"But first," Fiona Franklyn said, "you need a wrap-over skirt – easy to take off – and a blouse to go with it." That selection made, she got down to fundamentals. "Something very innocent and virginal, I think. Pink and white, perhaps. Of course, you're not as big around the bust as I am, but this bra was always too small for me. I don't know why he bought it except that it's very pretty. Strip off and try it on." She considered and discarded a suspender-belt. "The corselet, I think." She produced a dainty confection of lace and frills with attached suspenders. "What size shoes do you take?" Polly was allowed to discard her more mundane garments in the privacy of a luxurious bathroom. When she was dressed again down to very high-heeled, white shoes with anklestraps, they began to develop the act. Polly found herself entering into the spirit of the occasion and suggesting comic touches of her own. They laughed together until they cried. They broke off for a light meal and a chat in the early evening and then resumed. At first, Polly felt a shyness at showing herself in quite such seductive raiment even to another woman but it was impossible to feel anything but seductive in such a bedroom and when she began to visualise the whole scenario her sense of fun took over again. If she gave pleasure to others without being hurt . . . She made up her mind to enjoy herself, but as the appointed hour approached she could not escape a sensation of butterflies in the stomach.

Polly and Fiona had debated the choice of music at some length. Fiona had a large collection of records into which they had dipped. To break with tradition, they wanted nothing brassy. Sweet innocence was the order of the day. They toyed with Bach. They considered a recording of minuet music. But in the end they settled for John Lanchberry's ballet music from *Tales of Beatrix Potter*, and when the resident pianist had finished his virtuoso performance of the *Rhapsody in Blue*, he began to play the jovial melody of *Mrs Tiggywinkle's Laundry*. Polly made her entrance.

The small stage, with an even smaller dressing room on either side, occupied the further end of the big room. The stage was hung with a dark, velvety material. It was bare except for a small table and a slatted chair upstage and a similar chair near the footlights.

If she was nervous, nobody would have known it. Apparently unaware of any audience, Polly strolled across the stage, balancing carefully on the unfamiliar heels. Gaining confidence, she did a little dance step to the music, seemingly for her own pleasure. She detected a tiny murmur of surprise. This was not what they had expected. Polly took her time removing to the table a pair of lace gloves, her earrings and a necklace, all on loan from Fifi. Just as her audience was beginning to fidget, she unfastened and slipped out of the chiffon blouse and folded it carefully onto the upstage chair.

For another minute or two she fiddled with the rings on her fingers. One of them proved recalcitrant and she left it in place. She stretched and yawned. Then, in a single deft movement, she removed the skirt and laid it over the upstage chair on top of the blouse.

To the men in the audience she was beautiful. Even the women were captivated. One man later admitted that she portrayed so perfectly an innocent young girl accidentally intruded on that he felt impelled to look away. Polly had expected to feel embarrassment but instead she was aware of being an object of general male desire. The feeling was so novel and flattering that, after a suitably protracted interval, she removed the exquisite French panties with a degree of panache. Only a narrow, pink thong protected her modesty. The room was now silent except for the softly tinkling music.

Polly moved round the stage once more in her dancer's walk to drop the panties with her other clothing. She returned and lowered herself elegantly into the downstage chair. the lowered viewpoint allowed her to see through the stage-lighting and into the big room. From among a flowering of pink faces she managed to pick out Darryl at one of the side-tables and, standing near the back, Ronald Dent. It had been easy to disrobe while the audience were strangers and therefore of no account. In front of Darryl, in particular, she suddenly felt shy again. She closed her mind to the sensation and concentrated on remembering what had been rehearsed.

Polly leaned forward and reached behind her for the catch of her bra. The audience was expectant. But there was a long pause. She got to her feet and turned. The watchers could now see that the finger with the remaining ring was tangled with the laces at the top of the corselet. With a fixed smile, she struggled but to no avail. When the bra was unhooked at last and hung from her bent arm, her lovely young breasts were exposed but most of her audience was more concerned with her predicament. "Go and help her," one man hissed to his partner. "Don't be an ass," she retorted. "Can't you see that she's having us on?"

Polly could be seen to come to a decision. What could not be cured must be endured. She would finish the act somehow. She put her free hand to one of her suspenders but then remembered that the shoes would have to come off before she could remove the long, nylon stockings. She put a foot on the chair and, one-handed, managed to undo the buckle of the strap and extricate her foot. But when she stood, slant-hipped, and tried to take up the shoe the heel was seen to be jammed firmly between the slats. Polly frowned.

Still with one hand caught behind her back, she lifted the other foot and could be seen to try hard to keep the heel balanced on one of the slats, but with a sudden lurch the heel went down and jammed like the other. Polly raised her eyes to heaven and her lips moved. A rustle of amusement passed through the room.

There was only one possible solution. Polly tried to unbuckle the remaining shoe, but because the first shoe had been in her way she had put her foot rather close to the chairback and there was inadequate room for her hand to fumble with the buckle. In desperation, she reached between the slats of the chairback. But she could still not reach the buckle and when she tried to withdraw her hand it was firmly trapped.

By now, most of the audience had realised that she was clowning. When at last the pianist increased the pace and volume and she hopped and stumbled offstage, still attached to the chair by a hand and one foot, the laughter was drowned by a crashing outburst of applause. There were calls for an encore, but when Polly came out to take a bow she was wrapped in a towelling bathrobe. There were cries of disappointment but more applause.

When Polly was dressed and ready to face the world again – which entailed little more than resuming the few garments and the shoe that she had removed – the more compulsive of the gamblers had returned to the gaming tables and only a few remained to give her a smile and another, smaller, round of applause. But the Franklyns were waiting for her and drew her aside. "Did I do that all right?" she asked them.

"Surely you could feel that it was going well?" Mr Franklyn said. "They loved you. It made them slow to go back to the tables, but they'll be keen to come again."

"But I only did a few minutes."

He looked at his watch. "Twenty-five. Almost too long to interrupt the serious business of the evening. For the same fee, would you do two more Fridays?"

"The same act again? A joke isn't so funny, second time around."

"We can think up some variations," Fiona said. She shook with amusement. "How would you feel about getting dressed onstage this time, but things won't stay done up? Imagine it!" The two giggled together while Mr Franklyn looked on, smiling.

Polly told them that she would have to think it over. She made her excuses and walked down the room with a return of the fixed smile and as much dignity, she believed, as anyone could have managed. Her stride checked for an instant when she saw that Darryl had been joined at his table by the large figure of Ronald

190

Dent. Be natural, she reminded herself. She resumed her dancer's walk and concentrated on not turning an ankle on the high heels.

Darryl stood, one-legged, and managed to pull out a chair for her. "Well done!" he said. Dent seemed to feel that he was above the need for such courtesies. A bottle of champagne in a silver bucket had appeared.

"That was really something else!" Dent said. He poured from the bottle. His hand was unsteady and he was slightly flushed. Polly guessed that he had been drinking for some time. "You're good. I knew you was special when I saw you flatten Frankie Delrose, but I didn't know how special. Any time you want a manager, give me a call." The words were friendly. His mouth smiled but his usual scowl was still plastered across the upper part of his face and his eyes were savage.

Polly had a shrewd idea where such a call would ultimately lead. "Darryl's my manager," she said. "But thanks anyway." Darryl hid his surprise.

Dent squinted at Darryl. "He's a lucky lad. You're too good for him. I got a good mind to move in on you." Darryl stiffened and Polly saw his fingers flex. Dent must have noticed it also and remembered Darryl's profession. "But I wouldn't do that," he said hastily. He burped but tried belatedly to hide it behind his hand.

"I'm sure you wouldn't," Polly said, keeping her tone light. "You're too much of a gentleman." She lifted her glass to him and drank some champagne, fighting the bubbles.

"I wouldn't, not to Darryl. He's a friend. Aren't you, friend?" Having dragged the conversation to where he wanted it, Dent forced a smile. "Talking of friends, have

191

you seen that Diana lately, the one who used to live upstairs from you? Where's she staying?"

"No idea," Darryl said.

"I'm told that she's still around."

"That's so," Polly said carefully. "I passed her in the street the other day."

"Is that right?" Dent said. He frowned again, but this time in thought. "That's interesting. I want a word with her. If you see her again, try to find out where she's living and who with." He emptied the last of the bottle into their glasses. "I could be generous for a little help. I think that boyfriend of hers has something belonging to me. If she wasn't around any more, I'd be sure of it."

"She hasn't gone to him," Polly said. "She wouldn't. He's gone abroad and he beat her up before he left. She told me." Too late, she realised that this implied a closer relationship than she had meant to convey and tried to remedy the error. "There were bruises on her face when I met her, so I asked."

"Is that right?" Dent said again slowly. "When was that?"

"About ten days ago." Polly would have called her words back if she could. If Dent had seen the vase since Hugo Tyrone's flight abroad, she had as good as told him that the vase was still in the city.

Dent blinked at her thoughtfully as though filing her words away for later digestion. He made a signal to a passing waitress. "Time I wasn't here." He put a hand behind him, feeling for his wallet, then jumped to his feet and turned around. Polly saw that his hip pocket had been neatly slit and his wallet was gone. He rounded on Darryl and all his latent menace was in the open. "Did you do this?"

Darryl looked up at his towering figure. "God's sake," he said. "No. I don't go in for that. You can search me if you like."

Dent's voice was rising in volume. "You could have passed it to her under the table."

"He did no such thing. And you're not searching me without a fight. When did you last have your wallet in your hand?" Polly asked quickly.

The big man's face creased with the effort of trying to remember. Two of the security men – one of them a moonlighting wrestler from the gym – were approaching, drawn by Dent's raised voice. Mr Franklyn appeared as though out of nowhere. "Is there a problem?" he asked.

"My wallet's been lifted. But you know I'm good for the bill."

"You'd better come into the office and talk about it," Mr Franklyn said. Polly and Darryl made their escape.

Eleven

When she arrived home, Polly was still split between two contrasting emotions – surfing the crest of her debut in showbusiness (and trying not to wonder whether she had perhaps stepped over the bounds of proper behaviour), while at the same time she had an unhappy conviction that she had said too much to Dent. Even a mere glass and a half of champagne, coming on top of earlier spritzers and the euphoria of her successful performance, might have loosened her tongue and Ronald Dent, when he sobered up, might conclude that she knew much more than she had admitted.

Darryl, whom she consulted in the darkness after the light and their passion were both extinguished, was comforting. "You didn't suggest that Hugo had buggered off abroad two minutes after he finished roughing up his girlfriend. He may have left days later, taking the jug with him. If Ronnie Dent has the sense to read anything into what you said, which I wouldn't bet on, he has the sense to see that much. Good-night."

"That's all very well," Polly said, "but it's made him think about me."

"And what he's thinking about you, after tonight's

show, doesn't bear thinking about. Believe me, if he thinks about you at all he'll be seeing you in Fifi's undies with your tits hanging out. Same as I will. Good-*night!*" Polly flounced over in the bed and turned her back on him but she was not wholly displeased.

After much thought, she phoned the incident room number from the gym next day and left a message for DI Calendar to the effect that Daphne was worried and would he please make contact. It happened that Calendar was out and about that day and on the next he managed to take a Sunday off for the first time since the death of Patrick Mahon. On the Monday morning he was closeted with the Detective Superintendent who had overall charge of that and several other cases.

"We may have had the break we've been needing," Calendar said. "The pocket-slitter was picked up on Friday evening. A woman. She got away from one of my idiots but now at last we know what she looks like. And we have her bag of takings." He paused for dramatic effect. "In it was Ronald Dent's wallet."

"Any good?" asked the Detective Superintendent.

"Not a lot so far. There was a key, probably the key to a safe-deposit box, wrapped in paper and tucked into a corner, but there's no indication where it came from, let alone the number of the box. Hopeless, if we don't get more information. Credit cards – not all in his own name, which may give us grounds for pulling him in. His bank cards and a few club memberships. The usual odds and ends like credit card slips, which haven't conveyed much to us. About fifty quid in miscellaneous notes. And, in a new envelope, some brand new banknotes, large denominations, both pounds and dollars, to a total value of about a thousand."

"So he may have been preparing for a trip abroad?"

"Or to bribe somebody. Or somebody may just have paid him off. We've sent the lot to Forensic, in the faint hope that the boffins can find something useful. You remember we kept one piece of information to ourselves?"

"That Hains's body had been searched."

"Exactly. I'd hoped that something from Hains might turn up, but no luck so far. When they've done their bit, and if they haven't found anything of significance, we'll invite Mr Dent to come in to collect his property and see how he reacts. But the interesting thing is that he hasn't been seen anywhere around his usual haunts since early Saturday morning."

"You see a connection?"

"I'm hoping for one. Perhaps I'm being fooled by a coincidence, but it's possible that somewhere in that wallet there may be something incriminating that Dent's afraid we've seen and understood. And if that's why he's gone into hiding, his days are numbered. We've got somebody watching his bank, so, without his bank card and credit cards, he may soon be stuck for cash. He'll have to surface or pull another job. Either way, we should have him."

"He may have a stash somewhere – he's a slippery customer."

"I'm counting on his stash being in the safe-deposit box, and we've got the key."

"If it's the only one. I won't ask you who let the woman get away, but I hope you had his balls for breakfast."

The Detective Inspector nodded slowly. "What I'm really hoping for is to connect Ronnie Dent with one or both of the killings, as an associate if not the perpetrator. I know that it would be a change of style but I'd like to prove that he killed Hains."

"You were always the optimist," said his superior. "That's probably what keeps you plugging away. Good luck to you!"

That afternoon, Darryl and Polly were together in the tiny office when the phone rang. Polly picked it up and spoke.

"Darling, are you all right?" said a woman's voice.

"Mother?" Polly experienced a sudden pang of guilt but a moment's reflection satisfied her that the headmistress could not have gone on the warpath and phoned the mother because one of her ex-pupils had done a striptease in a gaming club. And, indeed, what any headmistresses did or said no longer had any relevance. Perhaps she should arrange for the story to be leaked back to her last school. The old biddy would have a heart attack.

"Of course it's your mother. Who else calls you darling? Don't answer that. When are you coming home?"

"I am home, Mother. Please don't make a fuss. I'm—" Polly broke off. She had been about to say that she was eighteen now, but Darryl was listening avidly. "I'm old enough to know my own mind. How did you get this number?"

She heard her mother laugh at the other end of the line. "You remember my friend Mrs Liston-Harper?"

"Nosy Rosie?"

"She means well. She's a fan of Frankie Delrose –
I think she fantasises about being ravished by him,
though God knows she's bigger than he is and that
face renders her pretty well ravish-proof. Anyway, she
taped a wrestling promotion but didn't have time to
watch it until a few days ago. She recognised you
immediately and was round in two jumps to show
me the video. It's taken me ever since to get a phone
number from the promoters. I always knew that you
were a bit of a tomboy but you surpassed yourself,
leaping into the ring and beating up wrestlers. Darling,
who is that nice-looking young man whose leg was
being pulled off?"

"Darryl Davidson."

"Darryl? He isn't Welsh, is he?"

"Not that I know. I'll ask him. He's with me now."
Polly covered the receiver. "Darryl, are you Welsh?"

"One of my grandmothers was," Darryl said.

"Only one of his grandmothers was," Polly told her
mother.

"That's all right then. If you're prepared to kick
heads in for his sake, I presume he means something
to you. I know you've passed the age of consent, but
you're still very young."

"I'm very mature for my age," Polly said with dignity.
She heard her mother laugh again. "I really am. I've
been earning my own living quite satisfactorily and
I am not, repeat not, coming home to live with you
anymore."

"I don't know that I'd want you to. You were
very hard work to live with, shockingly expensive
and usually disapproving as well. I just want to be
sure that you're all right and not making a ghastly

mistake. And I have a birthday present here for you."

"I'll accept a birthday present in the spirit in which it's offered," Polly said, "whatever that may be, but all I really want from you is my birth certificate, my passport and your blessing to get married."

"To the wrestler?"

"Try to think of him as a gymnasium proprietor and wrestling coach."

"Darling, I'm not as much of a snob as you're making me out. Is he good in bed?"

Polly considered and rejected several superlatives. "Yes, wonderful!"

"That sounds like a good foundation for a long and happy relationship. Of course you shall have those things. Tell me where to send them."

When the call finished, Darryl said, "I didn't know we were getting married. Or did you have somebody else in mind?"

She kissed him tenderly. "I'm telling you now," she said. "And if you let me down, what I did to Frankie Delrose will be nothing, absolutely nothing, compared to what I'd do to you. And you can't even run away until you've got your cast off."

"I wasn't going to run away. But you didn't give me a chance to ask you."

"I didn't see the point," Polly said. "You've only got one good knee and with that cast on you probably couldn't go down on that without rupturing yourself. And we both know that I was going to say yes anyway. What's more, it's your own fault for listening to other people's phonecalls."

*   *   *

A Running Jump

On the following afternoon, Detective Inspector Calendar found time to visit the gym. He had a private discussion with Polly in the office. When Polly had quoted as much as she could remember of her conversation with Ronald Dent, he stroked his chin. "I'm inclined to agree with your – er—"

"Fiancé," Polly said firmly.

"Fiancé." Calendar accepted the word after a glance at Polly's still ringless third finger. "I don't suppose that Dent's enough of a thinking animal to follow through. More to the point, he seems to have gone underground since shortly after you last spoke with him. There are a dozen possible reasons, but I have a hunch. Tell me, when he found that his wallet was missing, what was his reaction?"

"I told you. He tried to accuse Darryl of taking it."

"That was nonsense and he knew it," Calendar said. "What do you think his emotion was?"

Polly tried to recall the image of Dent's face at that moment. She found that she could see it clearly, the sudden sweat, the change of colour, the twitch of the mouth. "He was horrified. I didn't notice at the time because I was getting just as scared, but his reaction was fear."

"More than you would expect from the loss of a substantial but not enormous sum of money?"

Polly thought again. "Yes," she said at last. "Definitely. He wasn't just concerned at a loss. He was appalled." Polly shook her head. "Honestly, I thought he was going to pass out. It wasn't just shock, it was horror. Disaster. Clammy titty."

"*What?*"

"Sorry!" Polly said. "Just something we used to say at school. Calamity."

Calendar relaxed. "That's what I hoped you'd say. His immediate accusation of Mr Davidson was because his mind wouldn't accept the other possibility. He may even have seen the pickpocket arrested, which happened about when he'd be making his way to the casino, in which case he'd be even more sure that his wallet would come into our hands. I think there's something in it which will be the undoing of him. I don't know what yet, but I'll find out."

Detective Inspector Calendar hurried back to the incident room and phoned the second-in-command at the laboratory. "About that Dent wallet . . ."

"All done. Nothing of significance. Dent's own fingerprints all over everything, but you'd expect that. Nothing to interest you at all."

"There has to be something more. We have it on good authority that when he realised that his wallet was missing he looked like a man facing a clammy titty."

"A what?"

Calendar kept his face expressionless. Two constables in the room were grinning at him. "A calamity. Do it all over again, there's a good chap. See if there's dust traceable to the Mahon flat or the Hains killing. Look for a scrap of paper in the lining. Do you have the piece of paper the key was wrapped in?"

"We have it. Common or garden toilet paper, unused and unsullied."

"There's got be something. Got to."

A sigh. "All right. But you'll have to wait. There's

been a van robbery involving three cars and we're snowed under with urgent work. Is yours urgent?"

"Probably not as urgent as that. But do it as soon as you can, there's a good chap. I've a murder inquiry losing momentum."

Next day, what was to prove a day of reckoning ran its course, at first following what was becoming the due routine. Darryl had begun to help Polly with the garden in the late mornings, even beginning to ask questions and make suggestions. He had discarded his crutches and could manage with two sticks. Though the help he could offer was limited, Polly was happy to have him with her.

They lunched at home and then went by scooter to open up the gym. In the early evening Polly fetched a single portion of fish and chips, supplemented it with salad and served the larger portion to Darryl on the office desk. It was late when they both worked out in the gym, so that Polly could have the use of the showers after the clients had left and the cleaning was finished and so that Darryl could have the pleasure of watching her.

They had a last look round. Polly opened the door on the chain for a cautious peep into the outside world. There was nobody to be seen in her necessarily limited field of vision. When she removed the chain and reopened the door she was swept aside as a heavy weight barged against it, hitting her forehead. She staggered back, blinking away tears of pain.

Ronald Dent stood in the doorway, looking enormous against the dark outside. He slammed the heavy door behind him without apparent effort. His habitual scowl had burgeoned into an expression of fury, restrained for the moment but, lacking an intelligent mind in charge, unstable. His hair, even his rough clothes, seemed to bristle with it. Polly was in no doubt that it would take only a pinprick to cause explosion. The idea was doubly unsettling because Dent had in his hand a large, blue-black automatic pistol. It was pointed at Darryl and his finger was on the trigger.

"You lift either of those sticks and you're dogfood," he ground out. And to Polly, "You, go and stand beside him."

Polly moved slowly to Darryl's side. She could feel Darryl quivering with frustration. Her own knees were shaking and her head throbbed. She knew that Darryl was anchored by his injured leg. She told herself that she must stay calm and keep her wits about her but the only rational thought to come into her mind was that she hoped that Darryl would leave action to her. She stayed braced to make a sudden jump, but whether that would be in front of or behind Darryl she was unsure. She had a giddy idea that she might do both in the hope of saving both of them. Practicalities had slipped beyond her mind for the moment.

"I figured things out at last," Dent said. "Where is it?"

"Where's what?" said Darryl. He was the least feverish person in the room.

Polly had heard of the veins standing out on someone's temples but she had never before seen it happen. "The pot," Dent said. He was gripping the pistol so tightly that he might have crushed it.

Darryl, puzzled, raised his eyebrows as far as they would go. "Pot, as in dope?"

204

Polly thought that Dent was about to shoot. He took aim. Polly braced herself for a desperate attack along the lines of her assault on Frankie Delrose. It would be suicidal, but she did not want to live without Darryl. Dent pulled himself together just in time. "The jug. The Chinese vase," he gritted through clenched teeth. "Harry Hains was supposed to leave it in a locker at the station but he never did. He meant to make off with it. He brought it here and spent the next few days trying to get it away again without getting done over by a lot of fighters who still remember old Mahon. Everything's coming apart and the pot's my last chance if I don't want to start at the bottom of the pile again, and with my picture all over *Crimewatch*. So we're going to open the lockers until we find it."

"Okay," Darryl said, "if that's what you want. But you can't search the whole place on your own and the police already went through it like a plague."

Dent used a word that Polly had never heard before. "They figured out that much, did they? Did they find it?"

"Not that I ever heard."

Dent looked up into the dusty rafters where disused pipes and ducts silently attested to several previous industrial occupants. "No. They didn't find it or I'd have got the word," he said at last. "So that leaves just one other possibility. One of you two buggers found it. And you—" he pointed at Darryl "—were hopping around on crutches. I can't see you smuggling Chinese pots around under your coat. But you, sweetie-pie—" Polly felt the heat of his glare on her face "—you've got the nerve of the devil. I'm betting Darryl's life that you know where it is."

205

"I don't know anything," Polly said. Her voice seemed to come out in a mouse-like squeak. "Hugo Tyrome must have taken it out with him."

Dent waved the denial aside with the barrel of the pistol. "Hugo was already nabbed in New York while Harry was still trying to sneak back in here. So we're back where we started." His voice was rising again. "Doesn't matter which of you has it, or both of you. Doesn't even make any difference if neither of you knows nothing. It's too late for that. If I don't get the truth straight away I'm going to shoot lover-boy." He glanced at Polly and she was sure that she could see hot coals in his eyes. "And what I'll do to you then, darlin', won't be pretty. But one of us will enjoy it."

Polly was in no doubt that the threat was sincere. Terrible though the danger was to herself, the thought of somebody shooting Darryl was immeasurably worse. Moreover, given half a chance she could run for it and take a chance on a bullet, a half-chance that was beyond Darryl's reach. Concentrate on surviving, she told herself. There could be many a slip between the cup and Ronnie Dent's lip. She might even jog his elbow.

"When I said 'straight away'," Dent said grimly, "I didn't mean next week." He hefted the pistol. His face was the incarnation of malevolence.

"I took your bloody pot," Polly heard herself say. "It was in Harry Hains's locker." Darryl made a squeaky sound of protest.

"It's at your flat?"

Polly's wits had made a gradual recovery. Now she seemed to be thinking faster and faster. "No,"

she said. "Darryl didn't even know about it. It's in
the outhouse of an empty building. I could take you
there, but I definitely won't if you've hurt Darryl."

She flinched, expecting a titanic explosion of wrath,
but Ronald Dent seemed to consider the bargain an
equitable one. It seemed that he had come already
equipped for villainy. He felt in an inside pocket and
produced several nylon ties of the kind to be seen on
the gym's plumbing, the type which, she had been told,
had been used on the unfortunate Patrick Mahon.

"Turn your pockets out onto the apron of the ring,"
Dent told Darryl and, when that was done, "Over against
the wall," Dent told him. To Polly, "Put one of these
round lover-boy's wrist. Then the other through the
first and round that water-pipe and pull them tight."
When Polly seemed to be on the point of rebellion,
he added, "It would be quicker to shoot him." The
plain statement of fact was more frightening that an
outburst of fury. Polly complied in a hurry. Each
tie was a narrow, white nylon strap with a ratchet
buckle moulded into one end. Once pulled up, they
were almost impossible to undo but had to be cut.

"Bring the sticks away. Now fasten one strap round
your own wrist, put another through it and make a
loop and put your other wrist through, then hold
your hands out to me at arms' length." The unblink-
ing eye of the pistol gave Polly no margin for a
sudden attack. Flight would be useless while Darryl
was still captive and vulnerable. She obeyed with
shaking hands. Dent jerked the second strap tight
and took hold of Polly's upper arm. "Come along,"
he said. "And no tricks. Lover-boy will still be here,
remember, still standing on one leg. The sooner we

get this over the sooner you can get back here and comfort him."

Darryl found his voice. "If you hurt her one little bit, I'll come after you and kill you slowly."

"Yeah," Dent said. "You do that." He pulled the big door to behind them.

Polly had no intention of leading Ronald Dent to the vase. This determination was not due only to mere cupidity. If Dent got his hands on the vase, she was sure that he would not leave any witnesses alive behind him. Polly had the sublime faith of the young that nobody as unique as herself would be killed without being given at least one chance and that, given that chance, she would leap at it. In the meantime, survival remained the priority. She offered no resistance as she was led to where the bulk of a car loomed in the darkness of the yard and pushed into the front passenger seat. Dent fastened the seat-belt round her, outside her arms, seeming satisfied that this much restraint would at least slow down any sudden moves. When he slammed the door, the courtesy light went off. As he hurried round the car, Polly groped in the dark for the door handle but failed to find it.

Dent settled into the driver's seat. He tucked the pistol under his right buttock, where it was close to his hand but far beyond Polly's reach. She hoped that it might go off of its own accord and do him some serious damage but it was not so obliging. When he started the engine and switched on the lights, she saw that the driver's seat was forward so that his big frame was poised close to the steering wheel and that he was peering through the windscreen nervously, as though

unaccustomed to driving. He had had to fumble for
the key. Polly decided that the car was not his but
was either borrowed or stolen. He was surrounded by
a body odour which she had never noticed before and
he wore jeans and a dark sweater instead of the modest
suit and tie that had seemed to be habitual to him.
Ronald Dent, Polly decided, was sleeping rough.

"Which way?"

"To the right."

Polly had intended to grab the wheel as they left
the yard and try to make the car collide with the wall.
Then, perhaps, she could get out of the car and run,
or somebody would come to her aid or she could brace
herself and take whatever was coming to her. But her
first movement was too sudden. The inertia reel locked
her seat-belt. Dent noticed nothing. Polly decided that
it was better that way. It would be preferable to have
Dent a long way away from Darryl before making
a move.

The traffic was almost non-existent, so late in the
evening. They rolled along the street in glorious isolation.
The street lamps glistened on tarmac slick with light rain.
Polly leaned forward and raised her elbows slowly. The
car reached the first junction. The lights were green.
"Go left here," she said.

Two turns later she was off the streets that she knew.
She had to be careful and trust her sense of direction.
If she crossed or even approached their previous route,
Dent would know immediately that he was being led a
dance. By the same token, if she waited too long they
would find themselves in a cul-de-sac or approaching
open country. She became aware of another cause for
urgency. Dent had tightened the ties on her wrist to

the point where her hands were becoming numb. A few more minutes and they would be useless.

They rounded another corner. As they picked up speed again, Polly saw the blue lights of a police car approaching. She could still only reach the bottom of the steering wheel, so she chose her moment to grab it and pull with all her might. The car swerved. Dent pushed her off and fought to regain control, but too late. The skid was already established and his sudden stamp on the brakes made it more certain. They swerved across in front of the police car. The offside front hit a concrete lamp standard and the car stopped dead. Even before the impact, she had released the wheel and was struggling with the seat-belt but the catch defeated her. The police would have to hurry . . .

Polly's seat-belt, although she had gained some slack in it, saved her from hitting the windscreen. Dent was thrown forward, only to be punched back into his seat by the explosive inflation of the driver's airbag and firmly held there. At the same moment, the driver's door sprang open. The engine had stalled. Something clattered into the road.

The police car had stopped close by, its lamps illuminating the scene. Two policemen were approaching in haste. Polly held up her hands into the light so that they could see the bonds. "Be careful," she screamed. "He's got a gun."

The nearest policeman was a big man and hard-looking. He picked something out of the gutter and stooped to look into the car. "Well, well," he said. "Ronald Dent. The chiefs have been waiting for a word with you. We'll give you a lift to the station. You're nicked."

"On what charge?" Dent's chest was still squeezed by the airbag but he gasped the words out defiantly.

"Car theft for a starter. This car's on the stolen list. Taking and driving away. Joy-riding. After that, we'll see."

Polly showed her wrists again. "Abduction," she insisted.

"That, too," said the policeman. He looked at Dent. "Carrying off girls now, are we? Things go hard for sex criminals in the nick. Do me a favour, sunshine. Resist arrest."

"The gun," Polly reminded him urgently.

The policeman brought his hands up and Polly saw that he was holding the gun. "Air pistol," he said. "Not even loaded. Quite harmless." He used a small penknife to release Polly's hands.

Darryl tried shouting, but he knew the walls were too thick and the neighbours too far away. Then he tried force until he hurt his wrist and after that, guile. But nothing, it seemed, would separate him from the water-pipe. He heaved, trying to drag the pipe off the wall. Blood was running down his arm. He was on the point of resorting to prayer when the big door began to open. He held his breath. It could be Dent, coming back to kill him. But no, it was Polly returning to set him free.

He looked again. His eyes were deceiving him. This was not Polly. Unless she had aged suddenly, which was believable.

An elegant woman had entered. She had beautiful legs. Everything about her face and figure and the way she walked seemed familiar. She looked around

211

with eyebrows raised, taking in the dusty, masculine preserve. Then she saw Darryl and came forward, hand outstretched. "Good-evening," she said graciously. "You must be Darryl. How do you do? I'm Polly's mother. It seems that my daughter doesn't want to let you go."

Darryl, freed from his water-pipe by Polly's mother with the use of a pair of nail scissors from her handbag, was making an incoherent call to the police when a police car arrived at the gym with the news of Polly's rescue. Darryl was driven to the incident room and Mrs Turnbull insisted on being taken to see her daughter. She waited patiently (attended by several constables who should already have gone off duty) while the young lovers, individually, made statements. Polly told most of the truth and very little but the truth, but she still said nothing about the Chinese vase. If Darryl had a phobia about poverty then she would make sure that he never saw its face again.

DI Calendar had gone off duty but he hurried back as soon as word reached him. He spoke to Polly in private while her statement was being typed up, but he was not optimistic. "We can take Dent off the streets for a year or two. Car theft and abduction will do. But I'd have liked to get him for complicity in the death of Patrick Mahon and the murder of Hains. I'm quite certain that he changed the habit of a lifetime and dirtied his own hands in the Hains killing. But I can't see a jury convicting – I can't even see the DPP wanting to proceed – on the basis of oral evidence alone."

"Surely," Polly said, "his attempt to kidnap me has to be conclusive proof of his involvement."

"We'd still be relying on oral evidence to connect it up, and what he said to you would be hearsay. No, if we can't find any physical evidence, he'll be out again within a year. Two at the most."

Mrs Turnbull had reserved a room at the Coronet Hotel, but she accepted a lift with them in a police car to Darryl's flat. At first she sat looking around the spacious but shabby apartment, while between them they poured out almost the whole story to her. After a while she got up and stretched, saying that she had been sitting for most of the day. She went to lean against the mantelpiece. The spray of *cotoneaster horizontalis*, which Polly had renewed that morning, made a scarlet halo round her head. Darryl was captivated.

Polly returned to her original story. Her claim to Dent that she had the vase had been, she insisted, only a ploy to lure him away from Darryl and the gym and into the hands of the police. Darryl gripped her hand. When the story was finished, her mother asked a few questions but, like Polly, she was more inclined to look to the future than the past. "Quite an adventure!" she said. "But it's over now, please God." She looked at Darryl. "What are your plans?"

"I don't have plans," Darryl said. "I just roll along from day to day. Mostly, I leave plans to Polly."

"The perfect husband," Mrs Turnbull commented.

"I hope so," Polly said. "But I want whatever Darryl wants. Of course, we'll have to wait here for the court case and we could get married while we're waiting." She looked at Darryl. He was nodding happily. "And after that I had a sort of idea that

213

Darryl might like to settle in the USA, at least for a while."

Darryl stopped smiling. "God, no," he said. "Unless you really want to, that is."

"DI Calendar didn't think that Ronald Dent would be locked up for very long. And I'm not sure that I want to be around when he gets out. He's not going to like me as much as he did. A good wrestler can make money in the States," she added.

"I can deal with Ronnie Dent," Darryl said. "All right, you're thinking that I couldn't cope with him this evening—"

"I wasn't thinking any such thing," Polly protested. "If you hadn't had one leg in a cast, and if you'd known that the pistol was a dummy, you could have massacred him."

"Thanks. But, Polly, this is the place where I'm happy. I know the people and they know me. And we're not doing badly, what with the gymnasium and things. I hadn't realised how my savings were mounting up."

Polly sighed. She would have regretted leaving her garden, but the acquisition of wealth would have been less noticeable in an affluent foreign country. Darryl's happiness, however, came first. Perhaps Mr Shanks could be persuaded, and trusted, to make the trip.

"Then we'll stay here," she said. "When we can afford it, perhaps I'll go and take my degree after all. Mother, you'll have to help me choose wallpapers. And carpets and curtains."

This was a prospect after Mrs Turnbull's heart. "You must let me give you carpets and curtains as a wedding present, and a new suite. I insist, so don't argue."

"Who's arguing?" Polly asked. "You aren't, are you Darryl?"

"Not a lot, no."

"That's splendid!" Mrs Turnbull made a delighted gesture. Her shoulder caught the vase, which rocked, oscillated and fell into the hearth. Her last-moment grab saved only the branches and berries. The vase shattered into a thousand pieces.

"Oh dear!" breathed Mrs Turnbull contritely. "But never mind. It was quite hideous. I hope it wasn't valuable?"

Darryl looked puzzled. "I thought you said it was an heirloom?" he said to Polly.

"I was joking. It's all right, Mother," Polly said. "It was mine, but it didn't cost me anything." She fetched the dustpan and brush.

DI Calendar had had very little sleep and he was thinking through a layer of treacle when the message reached him. He was wanted at the police lab. His friend the deputy-chief was waiting for him. "We did it all over again," he said. "There are no prints that we didn't find first time around and no dust or fibres that correspond with anything in the Mahon or Hains cases."

Calendar yawned until his jaw cracked. "Did you have to fetch me all the way over here to tell me that?" he asked. "Let me tell you something. A chap named Bell invented the telephone. I think he also invented whisky."

"Very funny," said his friend without the least flicker of a smile. "But you said that Dent seemed horrified to have lost his wallet. I'm assuming that you haven't been able to trace any of the bank notes back to Dent or Mahon? So we had a bit of a think and it seemed to me that the one thing we'd been overlooking was the envelope the bigger notes were in. We'd already dusted it for prints, found some of Dent's and left it at that. Now we wondered if he hadn't been using it as a last resort *aide-mémoire*. So we tested it."

"And found something?"

"Invisible ink. Probably lemon juice. We only had to warm it up a little and the writing showed." The scientist handed over a paper. "This is a photocopy, we've got the original sealed for evidence. Whether it means anything or not is up to you."

Calendar looked at the photocopy. Sleep receded and he felt joy spreading through him. The small writing came at various angles, sometimes overlapping because the writer could not see his previous notes. It began with Patrick Mahon's address and continued with a detailed description and account of the Chinese vase. Below were several cryptic notes which only time would decipher, followed by several strings of numbers which he guessed to be overseas telephone numbers. Among the shorter numbers he recognised that of the gym and reference to his friend's telephone directory confirmed the number of the YMCA where Harry Hains had lived. Two other sets of digits he guessed were the number and combination of a safe-deposit box.

"What do you know?" he asked the ceiling. "It's going to take work, but between one thing and another . . . if we don't have the bastard by the short and curlies I'm going to retire and take up basket-weaving."

It took a week, but the safe-deposit was traced at last and DI Calendar visited the manager armed with

216

the key, the combination, the box number and a court order. The manager bowed to the inevitable and the box was opened. The contents were few and looked mundane. Calendar knew a moment of disappointment before he noticed that there were two passports. Even then, he nearly missed it. Men do keep two passports, not bothering to discard an old one or keeping it for an unexpired visa within. But when he came to open the second passport he struck gold. The passport had been issued to Harry Hains but Ronald Dent's photograph had been carefully inserted so that the plastic finish looked undisturbed.

Detective Inspector Calendar raised both fists. "Yes!" he shouted into the church-like silence. The other clients present in the vault looked shocked. "Got him!" he said more quietly.